The Lyon's Pride

Last night, I dreamed about Eleanor. It was a strange dream. In it, she was walking in a field of flowers, little Virginia running before her. Behind Eleanor walked a strange and shadowy figure. I thought it was Ananyas and heard her call out his name. Several times she called, but the figure remained shrouded in mist. She stopped at one point and began painting her name on the rough bark of trees. I don't know where the paint came from, but she dipped her fingers again and again in bright colors of red, blue and yellow. "Eleanor Dare," she wrote over and over, "Eleanor Dare."

The Lyon's Pride

M.L. Stainer

Illustrated by James Melvin

Chicken Soup Press, Inc.

Circleville, New York

Chicken Soup Press, Inc.
P.O. Box 164
Circleville, NY 10919

Library of Congress Cataloging-in-Publication Data
Stainer, M.L., 1939-
The Lyon's pride / M.L. Stainer ; illustrated by James Melvin
p.   cm. — (The Lyon saga ; bk. 3)
Sequel to The Lyon's cub.
Summary: When Eleanor Dare and others go off in search of the English colonists from the Roanoke colony, Jess and her family stay behind, building a new life with the Croatoan Indians and strengthening their interconnection when Jess and her "unqua" husband have a baby.
ISBN 0-9646904-8-9 (hc.). —ISBN 0-9646904-9-7 (pbk.)
1. Lumbee Indians—Juvenile fiction. 2. Roanoke Colony (N.C.)—Juvenile Fiction. [1. Lumbee Indians—Fiction. 2. Indians of North America—North Carolina—Fiction. 3. Roanoke Colony—Fiction.]
I. Melvin, James, ill. II. Title.
III. Series: Stainer, M.L., 1939- Lyon saga ; bk. 3.
PZ7.S78255Lv 1998
[Fic]—dc21   98-23980
                                                                    CIP
                                                                    AC

Book design by Netherfield Productions, Pine Bush, New York
Printed by Worzalla, Stevens Point, Wisconsin
10 9 8 7 6 5 4 3 2 1

To my friend, Myrna,

for always believing...

Other Works by M.L. Stainer

The Lyon's Roar (1997)
The Lyon's Cub (1998)

Contents

Author's Note

The author wishes to note that some spellings of familiar names have been changed according to how they are listed on original documents.

Croatoan is pronounced Cro-ah-tu-WAN; Manteo, MAN-tee-o; Ananyas, An-na-NEE-yus; Akaiyan, Uh-KY-yun; Towaye, TOH-way; Neusiok, NU-see-ok.

A special note of thanks to:

Robert Peay and Greg MacAvoy for their proofreading assistance: to Stella Denton of Pine Bush High School library and Fran O'Gorman of Goshen library, for their help in research: to Ricardo Carballal for his invaluable assistance with Spanish: to Harry L. Thompson, Curator of the Port-o-Plymouth Museum, Plymouth, North Carolina, for his encouragement: to my mother, Harriet Stainer, and my friends and family for their continued support.

Prologue

HISTORIANS AGREE that no one knows what happened to the Lost Colony of 1587. Some believe that the colonists, feeling abandoned by John White, split into two groups. The first headed north to the Chesapeake Bay, their original destination. The second group aligned themselves with the friendly Croatoan Indians and moved south to their island, making a home with Manteo's tribe.

Other historians firmly believe that some of the brave adventurers headed inland, toward what is now known as Georgia. Eleanor Dare was supposed to be among that group, leaving messages scratched on rough boulders along the way in the hope that her father, Governor White, would someday return to Roanoke and follow her.

Whether at Chesapeake Bay, Croatoan Island, or deep inland in search of others, these early explorers of our nation faced many dangers; hostile Indians and Spanish conquistadores constantly roamed through the areas of North and South Carolina and Virginia. There were dangers from disease, starvation and the unpredictable elements.

No one knows for sure what actually happened. Poetic

license allows the author to explore each possibility to its fullest potential.

Chapter 1

Preparations

AS I LOOK OUT on the preparations for leaving Croatoan Island, I wonder just how many times my heart can break. Eighteen of our brave colonists and friends have decided to leave the Indian village which has been our home for almost two years. The time of departure is at hand. Households have been packed, goodbyes said and now, tears aplenty are being shed. Christopher Cooper leads the new expedition with my dearest friend, Eleanor Dare, among them. Oh, how I shall miss her!

Sinopa herself comes down to the beach to bid them farewell. She's ruled well since the death of her sister and Manteo's mother, Shanewis. Towaye is coming with us, as is Akaiyan, Enrique and myself, to lead the brave adventurers once again up to Roanoak Island, then across the sound to the western mainland. Once there, they will move inland then turn south, heading down toward where they think George Howe and the others might be. It's a risky journey at best, but we're used to risks, we *nickreruroh*, as befits our English blood and backbone.

Once we see them safely across the sound and headed to the southlands, the four of us will return the way we came, back to Croatoan. Mother, Father and Thomas have decided to remain with our Indian friends, making this beautiful island their home, as it is mine already. Both Master and Mistress Steueens are staying, which pleases dear Mother immensely. Roger Bayley stays also, and Wenefrid Powell with her husband and babe, James.

Mother has refused to come down to the beach, to keep her heart from "rending in two," she says. For sweet Eleanor has been like a daughter to her, and a sister to me. Though we beg Eleanor to stay, her mind is made up.

"Think of little Virginia," Mother entreats. "You can't take her into the wilderness. What will become of you?"

Eleanor shakes her head sadly.

"Mother Joyce, there's nothing for me here. Ananyas lies in a shallow forgotten grave to the north; my unborn child is buried in an Indian field. For what reason should I stay?"

"For us, surely we're your family now? For your child, who needs the love of grandparents and relatives to hold her."

But Eleanor sets her mouth in a straight line and won't relent. Even I, who've been her closest confidante these many months since sailing from England, can't persuade her to stay with us.

"I'll miss you terribly," I tell her over and over again.

"And I, you."

"Won't you stay?"

"You mustn't ask again, dear Jess. For I've never been comfortable or truly happy here. I always wanted to go to the Chesapeake Baye. But... Ananyas... had his mind made up to stay. And now... he's gone and I must leave, too. I'm convinced we'll find George Howe and the others. We have all of my dear father's maps, those we can still read. The route's been plotted for us to follow. I'll leave markers, just in case you or your parents change your minds."

I run from her weeping, for this decision to leave unnerves me. She's never been as content here as I, refusing to dress little Virginia in buckskin, or participate in the *unqua* ceremonies.

Enrique tells me that some people need their own kind in order to live and grow, and Eleanor is one of these. She's remained steadfast in her desire to leave our village and journey south. The country is unknown and basically uncharted, except for a few notations on John White's maps. There are Indians living there of a different nature than the Croatoan, but whether or not they're friendly remains to be seen. They're of the Cherokee tribe and that's all we know.

Eleanor is confident that she and the others will find our English friends and neighbors from Roanoak. For George's letter had said they would head south, deep inland. And they, too, had seen the same maps. I hope and pray to Our Lord and Savior, Jesus Christ, that the two groups should meet and form as one again.

We're giving our brave friends one of the *a hots*. Enrique won't part with Diablo, the black stallion. Nor can we let Beauty go or her foal, Star, as each needs the other. So the second mare, Little Swan, has been chosen. Her pregnancy is in its earliest stages and she shouldn't come to term before they safely arrive. Enrique says it takes about eleven months for a horse's confinement, and she's only about one month now. Surely they'll arrive at their destination long before she gives birth. Though I'm terribly sad about her going, I know they'll need a horse to carry Eleanor and little Virginia on the long journey. And when she gives birth to her foal and it grows, the newly-joined colonists will have two swift animals to carry them far and wide.

Chapter 2

Enrique de Gomara

LITTLE SWAN EATS from my hands. She snorts gently into my palm. I scratch behind her ears, a favorite spot with all the *a hots*.

"Little Swan, I'm sorry to see you go. I wish I could see your babe born. But I know you'll carry Eleanor and Virginia safely to the southern lands."

Enrique is grooming Diablo. He uses a curry brush made of dried corn stalks. Diablo whinnies his pleasure. Every so often he stamps a hoof.

"That's just to let me know he's allowing me to groom him," laughs Enrique. "He always has to be in charge."

"I'm going to miss Little Swan," I say.

"Me, too. I've grown very fond of *los caballos, todos ellos*, all of them."

"Eleanor's leaving is a sad thing. How I wish her mind wasn't made up."

"I can see why she needs to go. For she has lost *su*

corazón."

I just stare at him. Such poetic words coming from my Spanish friend.

"What about you? Do you want to go, too?"

He gives a deep sigh.

"My home is across the wide sea.... But this place is beautiful. I could be happy here."

"The *unqua* like you. At first, they were terribly afraid, but then they saw what you were really like, instead of seeing just the uniform."

"I got rid of that *rapidamente.*"

And it's true. Enrique took his *soldado* uniform off that first week we returned, trading the gold braid and leather belt for buckskin garments. Indeed, he looks quite handsome clothed like the *unqua.* He's pulled his long brown hair back in a tail, like Akaiyan, and stuck an eagle's feather there. If it weren't for his boots, he could pass for a Croatoan, for his skin is dark already from the hot Spanish sun.

He rests his hands on Diablo, whispering in the stallion's ear.

"What are you saying?"

"That I think he is *mágnifico*, the greatest *caballo* in all the known world."

"But what about your uncle's horses back home?"

"They're *mágnificos* also," he laughs, "but I am here and they're across the sea. So Diablo is now the greatest...."

We both laugh. Star pushes at me with her nose. I pet her absent-mindedly.

"Do you want to go home?"

He stares at the sun rising in the eastern sky, streaking the horizon with pink and gold. A look of pain comes to his face.

"I long for my mother and sisters. It's been almost three years now that I haven't seen them. Gabriela must be about twelve, and Margarita is fifteen. My mother is growing older.... And what of your home back in England?"

"This is my home now," I state firmly. "Though I'll never forget my English roots. I love the *unqua*, their gentleness, their love of nature."

"*¿Te casarías con Akaiyan?*"

I blush furiously and then say with much boldness,

"I hope we'll marry soon."

I watch now as Enrique and Akaiyan prepare Little Swan for her journey. A soft saddle is placed upon her back, with bags for carrying food and clothing. The *unqua* have fashioned a travois, made of two long poles with deerskin to join them. Goods of all kinds can be placed on the travois as Little Swan pulls it, attached to her saddle with the ends of the long poles dragging on the ground behind her.

Enrique plans to take Diablo also, for us to ride part-way, and for protection against any strange Savages we might encounter. The Weapemeoc's frightened reaction when they first saw Enrique riding him was sufficient to let us know how valuable he'll be keeping unknown hostiles at bay.

"To them, he's a monster, a *demonio!*"

"From *popogusso*, hell!" I laugh in return.

I watch as Enrique croons to Little Swan, stroking her nose and rubbing her ears. How lucky we are to have him! What a good friend he's becoming!

Akaiyan pulls me to one side where we're alone. "I want you to be my *kateocca*, wife, before we leave."

I shake my head.

"Mother and Father will never allow it."

"Do you wish it?"

My answer is a kiss of the most passionate nature. He pulls me close, his voice husky with burning fire.

"If not now, then when we return. I cannot wait much longer."

But I don't tell Mother a thing. She's upset enough that I'm once again leaving what she calls "our safe haven."

"Our route is different this time, dear Mother."

"But there are still Savages out there. And probably Spanish soldiers as well."

"*Los soldados no nos molestarán*," I reply, slipping easily into the Spanish tongue. "They won't bother us," I translate. She stares at me long and hard.

"You've changed so much."

"Yes, I'm not the child I once was." Then I give her a hug.

"But I'm still your little girl."

She looks away from me at my father, who says nothing.

"You're an *unqua* now," she whispers, using the Indian term. "And I hardly know you any more."

Chapter 3

Saying Goodbye

INSIDE HER LODGE HOUSE, Eleanor is making final preparations for departure. All of little Virginia's clothes are bundled up. Eleanor has packed her household goods, such as she'll need, and her clothing as well. She moves methodically through the small room, checking everything. At length, she turns and hands me her volume of stories.

"Here, this is for you, sweet Jess. I know how much you like to read. I'd give you my Holy Bible, but it was lost when you were captured."

Tears are running down my cheeks, and hers as well.

"What shall I do with Ananyas's rocking chair that he made me? I'd love to take it, but surely it won't fit on the travois."

It's as if she's talking to herself, as if I'm not standing there before her. She moves and sits down upon it, rocking slowly back and forth, smoothing the wood with her hands.

"Such a beautiful chair. He worked so hard. It took him

many months...."

Little Virginia tugs on my skirt.

"See, see," she says, holding up her rag doll.

"Why, she's so pretty," I answer, pretending to kiss the doll. She giggles delightedly.

"I know," says Eleanor, suddenly rising up. "You can have the chair. For soon you'll be married, isn't that true?"

I blush, for I've told no one of my plans to wed Akaiyan. Indeed, I don't know yet how Manteo will feel about our joining, and Mother and Father definitely will be opposed.

"I'm not married yet," is all I can think of to say.

"But I know your heart better than you imagine. You're quite obvious, my dear Jess."

"Would it be so wrong to... marry him?"

"In whose eyes?" she wisely asks.

"Not in mine. But Mother... Father, even Manteo himself...."

"Life is short," she whispers sadly. "And when we least expect, it takes from us those we love. I had years of happiness. I wouldn't part with them for anything. You must follow your own heart, Jess, and not anyone else's."

And so we embrace, each one's tears mingling with the other's as we weep. For Eleanor has been more than a friend, a true sister of my heart. I can't put into words the depths of my feelings for her.

"I'll say prayers daily for your safe trip. Don't forget me."

"I could never forget you," she says, breaking anew into sobs.

"You could change your mind and stay."

But she shakes her head.

"I'm not like you, Jess. This can never be my home."

I go outside then, leaving her to finish packing. My heart

is breaking and I head directly to the horses, to say yet another goodbye to Little Swan.

Surprisingly, Father is standing by her stall, stroking her broad rump. He turns when I enter.

"You've been crying?"

"I was with Eleanor, watching her pack."

"This is a sad day," he comments. "Your mother and I wish you weren't going with them."

"Not even as a guide?"

"We almost lost you once. We don't want to lose you again."

"Father," I start to say, then can't. He holds out his arms and I go to him, leaning my head upon his shoulder.

"You're back from the dead. I can't bear your leaving again."

"We won't be gone long," I whisper. "Just long enough to see them safely across the sound and headed south."

"We had a hard time keeping Thomas from going with you. He's growing up before my eyes. I'm afraid he's almost as headstrong as you, dear Jess."

He begins to laugh, then breaks into a fit of coughing. To my great alarm, I see blood flecking his lips.

"Oh, Father," I cry, "what is this blood?"

"'Tis nothing," he answers. "Don't tell Mother, whatever you do."

"But...," I start to say. He puts a finger to his lips.

"She has enough to worry about. Promise...."

I nod my head, holding him closely. I can feel that he has grown much thinner. His hair is quite grey.

"I'll hurry back, I promise. We'll be careful."

He leaves then, and I watch him walk slowly back to our lodge house. How did my beloved father get this way? In the blink of an eye, he's become an old man. I bite my lip to keep from crying anew.

Chapter 4

Words Of Wisdom

"I WISH I COULD GO WITH YOU."

The deep, familiar voice sings like music in my ears. From fearing Manteo, I've grown to honor and respect him. It was he who first spoke in the Croatoan tongue to me and, to my great delight, I was able to answer. From that moment on, I was no longer *werricauna*, afraid; no longer a foolish child as I'd been on our voyage across the mighty western ocean.

Even so, my heart leaps within my breast. For it's rare that he leaves his meditations and his dealings with the tribe. With my heart pounding, I turn to face him.

"I'm honored that you come to see me."

"You are no longer *woccanookne*, a child, but a *connoowa*."

I nod my head in recognition of his calling me a woman.

"I watched you from the beginning," he says slowly. "My son is also no longer *wariaugh*. He wishes to marry you."

My face is, no doubt, the color of summer berries. I don't

know how to answer him. Finally he nods his head.

"It is a good thing, this joining. I have given it much thought. It will bond the *nickreruroh* and *unqua* together. What does your father say?"

"I think it's my mother who will be the most displeased. My father isn't well."

"I have noticed the *nauwox*, sickness, within him. He has *utchar*, fire in his chest. Even Towaye cannot drive it out."

"I think, perhaps, my father may die. He's become an old man, *occooahawa*, before my eyes."

Manteo nods his head. He turns to leave but then, faces me once again.

"When will this marriage take place?"

In my most immodest way, I blurt out,

"I wish it could be now.... But we'll wait, until we return."

He holds out his hand. Resting in his palm is a wooden carving. He nods as I take it.

"This is for you. It is a symbol of the *a hots* which you have brought us, as a gift to my people. They are a great gift. I would wish that we had ten of them, *wartsauh*."

The carving is of a small horse rearing upon its two hind legs. The wood is highly polished and must have taken days to make. My eyes fill with tears. It's the first *unqua* present I've ever received, except for the amulet around my neck that Akaiyan gave me.

"I shall treasure this gift."

"Little Bird," he says then, "you have given my son much joy.... I shall be glad when you marry with him. But you must be careful on this journey. You must watch for the *auk-noc*, guns of the... Spanish; you must watch for the *oosocke nauh* of the enemy...."

His voice is low and full of a subtle anger. I can see the

blood pulsing in his temples.

"Many Croatoan have been killed while hunting... not all *unqua* are *caunotka*, brothers."

"The Weapemeoc...?"

He nods.

"Those, and... others...."

He leaves as silently as he had come. I watch as he walks slowly back to his lodge house. Even he looks older than I remember. It seems then that as I grow in knowledge and understanding, those I care for and love age before my very eyes. Why does that have to be so? Why is there so much that I still don't understand? More than anything, at this moment, I long to be a little child again, running and playing with my friends, laughing as if the world were a happy place, instead of one filled with anguish and unknown dangers. If I could wish for anything, it would be that my beloved father be young and well again, that Ananyas was dancing with Eleanor in his arms, that Mother didn't look so worried all the time, that Margaret and Dyonis Harvye were still with us, that Agnes hadn't died....

"You're so deep in thought. Should I be worried?"

And there is Enrique, saddling Diablo and making ready for our departure, getting ready to lead Little Swan down to the sandy beach. I toss my head and smile.

"I was just wondering where Akaiyan is?"

"Helping Towaye with supplies, *para nuestro viaje*, for our journey."

"Will we be all right?"

I grab his arm suddenly. He looks puzzled, then breaks into a smile.

"I thought you were *una conquistadora valiente*, without fear."

15

"I am afraid," I confess softly. "But I mustn't show it."

Enrique makes the sign of the cross. I quickly follow.

"*Dios Mío, Jesús Cristo*, watch over us and guide us on our journey. May we return safely once more to this *isla bella*, and to those who love us."

Chapter 5

Farewell To Roanoak

THE JOURNEY NORTH to Roanoak is uneventful. Eleanor and Virginia ride Little Swan, the travois behind her loaded with bundles. Because of this, she moves slowly. Christopher Cooper leads her by rein, while the rest of us walk alongside. Enrique rides Diablo, keeping a firm hand on him, for the black stallion wants to gallop. Only Towaye and Akaiyan scout ahead, making sure the way is clear. We have crossed the narrow channel safely in several *ooshunnawa*, while Little Swan and Diablo swam behind. I'm worried about Little Swan, for I wouldn't want her to miscarry her unborn foal.

We move up the outer banks of land. It's our plan to reach the point where we're parallel to Roanoak Island, then once more cross over. The *ooshunnawa* are cumbersome to carry, but necessary. The colonists move with a glad heart, for all who brave this venture are glad to leave the *unqua* and seek out other Englishmen. I can even hear Eleanor humming softly to Virginia as they ride. It's the first time on an *a hots'* back for the little girl; she clutches Little Swan's mane and holds on tightly.

We stop and rest many times, giving us a chance to lay down our burdens and gather strength. It's a much slower trip than when we rode down, just Enrique, Akaiyan and myself. I know that Enrique has trouble keeping Diablo in check. The black snorts his displeasure at being held on such a short rein. Many times he tries to grab the metal bit between his teeth.

It takes us almost three days just to reach the point opposite Roanoak. We sleep under the stars each night and the weather holds fair. It's the beginning of April and the air is fresh with the scent of new growth. The sea rolls its waves on our right. One day we detour onto the sandy beach and let the *a hots* walk at the water's edge. I look across the mighty expanse of water, wondering what lies on the other side. Is it my fair England, or Enrique's homeland or even, perhaps, the dark mysterious lands of Africa? I remember our days upon its vast depths, storm-tossed and often sea-sick. Will I ever be brave enough to venture across a second time? I don't know the answer to that question.

The crossing to Roanoak is more difficult. The channel is broader and the tide rushes in. The *a hots* have a harder time. I'm glad for Little Swan and Diablo when we finally touch Roanoak's sandy shore. Akaiyan has told me we'll build a raft and float them across the water separating us from the western mainland. I wonder how they'll like standing on a surface which rocks back and forth under their hooves.

We're almost directly across from our original encampment. Eleanor hasn't seen the ruin it's become and she gasps, her hand flying to her mouth, when she walks through the overgrowth of weeds, viewing the structures in such disrepair. She slowly enters the house she once shared with Ananyas.

None of us follow. When she emerges, we can see she's been crying.

John White's possessions still lie strewn about, more in ruins than ever. Several of the men start picking through the charts he left behind, seeing if there's anything to salvage. But we'd taken all the ones earlier which hadn't been damaged by wind, snow or rain.

"There's nothing of value here," Christopher Cooper says dismally, and sets off to examine the timbered house he'd once occupied. Some of the others do the same. I walk silently to the three crosses on the edge of the clearing, though bushes and vines have now entangled them. I clear away the brush and feel a tear trickle down my cheek upon reading the words: "Here Lies Agnes Harvye, born 1580, died 1587." John Tydway's marker lies just beyond, and so does the one for George Howe, the elder. It's too much to bear. I place wildflowers on each of the grave sites, then get up hurridly and return to the *a hots*, to Enrique and Akaiyan who see my anguish but say nothing.

And so we move on, across Roanoak to the western shoreline. The men set about felling trees and stripping branches to make a raft of sizeable proportions. We eat and make ready for the night. We'll leave by earliest light.

I'm awakened by the sounds of many birds, all welcoming the coming of springtime and the season of renewal. Already the men are working on the raft, roping the logs together, making the knots firm and tight against the salt water.

"Will it hold *los caballos*?" I ask Enrique. He smiles wryly.

"I hope so. Or *van a tener que nadar mucho*, they're going to have to swim a lot."

The channel to the western shore is deeper and longer than the one we crossed earlier. Though it's the sound, it's still further than we'd like the *a hots* to have to swim. Diablo is strong but my concern is still for Little Swan. My thoughts fly to Beauty and Star back on Croatoan Island. How I miss them!

Enrique, Akaiyan and Master Rufoote will ride the raft with both horses, holding fast to each one. The animals have been blindfolded. Diablo rears several times, but Little Swan remains calm. I'm thankful for her patient disposition. The men and women get into the *ooshunnawa*, as do Eleanor, Virginia and myself. The raft is fastened behind us, to be towed by three of the canoes. It will take great strength for the men to pull the raft with all its weight. Enrique leads *los caballos* into the shallow water, then up onto their floating ship. The motion makes them both afraid. There's much snorting and their hides are quickly lathered.

Enrique and Akaiyan push the raft out into deeper water, then jump aboard. I watch them all the way across, staring as the shoreline of Roanoak recedes and the mainland looms closer and closer.

Chapter 6

Heading Inland

WE'VE BEEN TRAVELING for six days now, through brush and undergrowth which impedes our progress. This is uncharted land to me and Akaiyan, and certainly to Enrique, whose knowledge of the New World has been limited only to the seas surrounding it, the Spanish garrison at Chesapeake and Croatoan Island. The men and women of this venture have ceased smiling, weary with hacking through the thick bushes and brambles.

Little Virginia frets often and it takes all of Eleanor's skill to keep her occupied and quiet. For we don't want any loud noises to ring out through the woodlands and alert a hidden enemy. The child plays with ribbons and necklaces that Eleanor has packed as toys. Her favorite rag doll sits in front of her upon Little Swan's broad back, riding as if she owned the world. Whenever Virginia's tired, Eleanor places her in one of the side baskets, especially lined with soft hides to keep her snug and warm. It's only when Virginia is sleeping that Eleanor relaxes and closes her eyes as she rides, the mare's rocking movement soothing not only her child, but Eleanor herself.

As for me, Enrique has let me ride Diablo on several occasions, noticing when I'm tired and lagging behind. He holds the reins tightly as he leads the black stallion through the trees while I, upon his back, delight in the chance to rest my legs. Akaiyan scouts ahead and to either side, always listening, ever alert to unknown dangers. The men on this brave expedition follow his lead, walking carefully at the ready for any possibility. John Chapman and his goodwife, Alice, walk close to Eleanor who, whenever she notices that Mistress Alice is tired, gladly offers her a chance to ride. She does the same for Mistress Payne, whose husband Henry is a big man with a long stride. Little Rose Payne almost has to run to keep up.

And so we move slowly southward, wending our way through tall pines and thick grasses. We've seen no sign of hostiles of any kind, and I wonder if we've entered the territory of those Indians called Cherokee. There's little known about these *unqua*, and whether they're friendly or hostile is a question as yet unanswered.

On the eve of the seventh day, Henry Rufoote twists his ankle badly, stepping into some sort of animal's burrow. He goes down with a cry of pain. We pull the horses to a halt and dismount. Mistress Payne, who knows doctoring of a sort, hurries to see the damage. His ankle is beginning to swell, so she wraps it in tight cloth and bids him rest. Since the sun is almost setting, we take advantage of the day's end and make provision to camp.

I've noticed that Eleanor has taken the opportunity at each stopping-place to make a mark. She does so by scratching upon the surface of a boulder with a sharpened rock that she carries tucked in the fold of her skirt. This time, I watch as she again scratches upon a large rock near our makeshift camp.

"What do you write upon each boulder?"

"My name, the date, and our direction. This way, whoever wishes to follow us will know the path we've taken."

I peer over her shoulder to see what she's written. Sure enough, in thin but distinctive lines the markings read,

'E. Dare, six April, 1589.'

"On this one, I shall leave a message," she says, busily scratching. When she's finished, I can read her note, carved in roughest stone,

'Father, been 2 years. I am well.'

"He'll know it's you," I say, "should he come this way."

"He'll come," she avows firmly. "Sooner or later, he'll return to Roanoak. I left him a message there."

"I didn't notice. What did you say?"

"Father, we head inland. Follow. April 2. E.D."

I leave her busily to her task, my heart heavy. For I wonder, as I've often wondered, if John White will ever return to the New World. Perhaps his ship had been fired upon by a Spanish pirate; perhaps it had sunk beneath the wild waves; perhaps he never arrived back in England; perhaps.... I shake my head to clear it of such thoughts.

Hands seize my shoulders and I gasp, my heart skipping a beat. Is it *soldados*, or hostiles? But then, I'm spun around and find myself staring into Akaiyan's eyes. He smiles and I smile back, so relieved am I that it's he. He pulls me close in an embrace, his skin warm against mine. I can feel his heart beating in rhythm with my own.

"You were lost in thought."

I nod my head. He kisses me deeply, as if trying to draw the breath from my body. I kiss him back unashamedly, for who's to see in these wild, untamed woods. Only Eleanor, and her back is to us in her endeavor. Akaiyan pulls me to the ground, his hands once again seeking, touching as he'd done back on Croatoan Island. I'm burning with a fire that leaves me breathless. His hands move over me, his mouth is on mine, and I'm sinking, sinking....

Chapter 7

"I Can't Bear To Leave You."

THAT EVENING by the fire's light, I think with burning cheeks upon Akaiyan. It was only by sheer force of will that I was able to restrain myself, for I wanted him to love me as much as he wanted it. But my joining with him won't be on an earthy forest floor, I swear it. I'll have a proper nuptial bed after a proper marriage ceremony. I owe my dear parents that much. I pushed him away and sprang up, brushing the dirt from my clothes, my face red, my breathing still heavy. His look was one of pain, of longing, but I steeled my heart.

"We can't," was all I said. I think he must feel that all *nickreruroh* are crazy people. He went then to help Towaye and Enrique. I turned to see Eleanor still absorbed in her task, leaving messages for her father, for anyone who might follow in our footsteps.

We travel on, day after endless day, leaving markers on boulders, seeing no sign of Spanish, of hostiles. Little Swan plods along; Diablo chomps the bit and frets to be set free to gallop. At one point we come to an open meadow, laced with budding yellow flowers. The way is clear according to Towaye. We pause on its edge and watch as Enrique gives free rein to the black stallion. Diablo gallops across the field, throwing clods of dirt from his hooves. Enrique gives him his head, guiding him only with his knees, as he's learned from our *unqua* friends. Round and round, across and back again, the stallion races to his heart's content. When at last Enrique pulls him up, the black is lathered and quiet, his head lowered, his nostrils flared with his breathing.

"He needed that," I say to Enrique in Spanish and then, the same thing to Akaiyan in Croatoan. The *nickreruroh* watch the magnificent animal in silence and awe. Even Virginia is enthralled, clapping her hands when Enrique trots him over.

Akaiyan looks at the sun high in the sky.

"It's here that we should leave them," he says to Towaye and me. I translate for Enrique, who nods his head.

When I tell Eleanor and the others, Mistress Payne begins to cry, putting her head in her hands and weeping most copiously. I see that Eleanor is trying hard not to cry also. Indeed, it's all I can do not to follow suit.

"I can't bear to leave you," she says at long last. "Surely, we haven't reached the half-way mark?"

"Not yet," answers Henry Rufoote, still limping slightly from his bandaged ankle. Though the swelling has gone down immensely, if he stands too long it begins to hurt again.

"We've days to go 'til we reach half-way. And who knows what half-way is," he laughs. "Who knows where exactly we're going."

Mistress Payne gasps, plopping down suddenly upon the ground.

"I thought we were meeting George Howe and the others."

She begins to weep again.

"We are, dear goodwife, but where they are, we're not sure. We've been heading in their general direction, following John White's map. But 'tis a long way to go, and they could have detoured in any direction."

Her weeping continues.

"We're lost," she gasps between sobs, wringing her hands.

"No, we're not," states Christopher Cooper firmly. "We follow the same route they've taken, I'm certain of it."

There's much debate. The men talk in small groups; the women gather around Mistress Payne and fair Eleanor. Akaiyan, Towaye, Enrique and I wait our distance. Eleanor turns suddenly to us.

"Won't you come with us just a little further?" she entreats. "For surely we'll be lost without your guidance."

"The *unqua* don't know these lands," I speak for them. "Virginia is a big territory. They only know we're close to the land of the Cherokee. Towaye met some once."

They all turn to look at Towaye. I speak to him in Croatoan.

"Tell them about the Cherokee you met. Tell them what they were like."

As Towaye speaks, I translate.

"The Cherokee call themselves the *Ani-Yunwiwa*, real people. They live in the mountains and foothills of these lands. They're peaceful, hunting only for food. They gave me presents of many *coona*, turkeys and *cotcoo*, ducks. I showed them *oosquaana*, a tobacco pipe, and how to *oo-teighne*, smoke."

Towaye shrugs.

"That's all he knows," I say.

"That's not much to go on," comments Christopher Cooper. He turns to the others.

"At least they're peaceful."

"How does he know for sure?" Alice Chapman asks, staring boldly at Towaye. He stares back. She drops her eyes and retreats behind her husband's back.

"Well, they didn't kill him," Henry Rufoote laughs a loud, hearty guffaw. The rest of us can't help smiling.

Chapter 8

"Just A Little Further."

TWO MORE DAYS and nights pass as we move deeper into Cherokee territory. We've seen signs of hunting parties, but no actual Indians. Akaiyan and Towaye scout vigilantly ahead, signaling us when to move and when to wait until the way is clear.

The buds are giving way to spring flowers before our very eyes. Riotous colors and smells assail our senses. Reds, yellows, blues, purples peek from beneath rocks and behind fallen tree trunks. The air is filled with the scent of honey. I think this is the same sweetness I smelled as we passed the islands while sailing through the West Indies on our passage here. As we move further south, the flowers bloom more profusely. Nature is bountiful in the springtime, as generous in her array as she's harsh and stark in her winter. I give silent thanks that Eleanor and the others will be traveling and settling eventually in a land of beauty.

Eleanor walks beside me often, letting Alice Chapman,

Rose Payne and some of the others take turns riding Little Swan. The women are more afraid of her than Eleanor, especially little Mistress Payne. Her husband lifts her and swings her high onto the mare's broad back. Mistress Payne gasps and looks for a moment as if she might swoon. But instead, she grips Little Swan's mane with iron fingers until we can persuade her to relax.

"Just hold the reins lightly in your hands," I tell her. "Little Swan is a gentle animal. She won't gallop."

"I'll fall right off if she does," avows Mistress Payne, but she does what I tell her. Once accustomed to the sway of the mare's gait, she proceeds to enjoy herself.

"I've never been this tall," she states emphatically and we all laugh.

Akaiyan keeps telling me we must leave them to go ahead, while we turn back. I know in my heart that that's true. For we've been gone too long already. Father and Mother will be beside themselves with worry. On the morning of the third day, Towaye and Akaiyan turn to Christopher Cooper, with me as translator, and tell him we must now depart.

This time, in spite of much weeping and heartfelt sorrow, we kiss all the women goodbye and shake hands with every man. Eleanor is sobbing silently, her shoulders heaving.

"Do you wish to come back with us?" I ask, biting my lip in the hope she'll say yes. But she shakes her head, and asks simply,

"Just a little bit further?"

When I stand there without moving, she hugs me long and hard.

"I'll leave you markers should you ever wish to follow," she says softly, then walks slowly back to the others, holding little Virginia's hand. I've already smothered the child in kisses and given her my final gift, a soft new rag doll I made back on Croatoan Island. She hugs it tightly to her chest as she turns to wave again and again.

I've kissed Little Swan on the nose, leaning my head against her broad sides. Already I imagine I can feel her foal growing big and strong inside her.

"God's grace upon you and your babe," I whisper in her ear. She blows her warm breath into my palm.

"God's speed, God's grace to all of you," I call, "for I know you'll find George and the others," waving until my arm will surely separate from my body. We watch as the small brave group moves off into the trees. My eyes water with the strain of watching, until the tears I shed are a mixture of strain and sorrow at yet another sad goodbye. England's brave lyon cubs have scattered to the winds, and now all she has left is her fierce, indomitable pride. Will we ever bring her true glory, I wonder?

I shall miss Eleanor and Virginia the most, for she was as a sister to me all these months and years. I'll miss the child, with her smiling face and laughter. I'll miss them all, I think, and Little Swan, whose gentleness is the exact opposite of Diablo. The black stallion paws the ground impatiently, anxious to be at a gallop. Enrique asks,

"Do you wish to ride?" but I shake my head, preferring at this time to walk hand in hand with Akaiyan, while Towaye slips ahead into the trees.

Not a word is spoken, for my heart is heavy. I know that I'll probably never see sweet Eleanor Dare again, nor Virginia. I find it hard to breathe until Akaiyan seizes me around the waist and lifts me off the ground, to bring me down and kiss me hard.

"Do not be sad," he says with a smile, "for *ki you se*, a

thousand joys await us back home."

I grab his hand and push aside the tears which threaten to drown me. For Eleanor has made her choice, to join once more with her own English folk, and I've made mine; to bond with the *unqua* and live their way of life, to be the wife of Akaiyan and the mother of his children.

Chapter 9

Spanish Soldados

WE STUMBLE UPON the *soldados* and the Cherokee two days into our journey northeast. The trees are thick and the brambles pull at us. Diablo's hide is pricked with flecks of blood from all the thorns. He sidesteps nervously. Enrique dismounts and blindfolds him. Immediately, he ceases his fretting and lets himself be led by hand. At that moment, Towaye slips back to us. Where he's been, I don't know, for he's always ahead or to the side of us. This time, instead of waving us forward, he puts a finger to his lips.

"Quiet," he whispers in Croatoan, "danger ahead."

We stop and Enrique places a calming hand upon Diablo's nose. As long as he's blindfolded, the black will remain docile. Akaiyan and Towaye speak rapidly, too low for me to understand. At last, Akaiyan turns to me and Enrique.

"Spanish uniforms," he mutters, "and Cherokee. Talking together. *Katichlei*, rogues."

I strain to see, but Akaiyan pulls me low to the ground.

Enrique hands the reins to him, and follows Towaye into the trees. Akaiyan tethers Diablo and keeps stroking him, soothing him so the great stallion won't make a sound. We wait for an interminable length of time. At long last, Enrique returns.

"*Soldados*," he says, "making deals with the Cherokee. *Son desertores del ejercito*, deserters, offering the Savages many beads for knives. They argue, and there is whiskey and rum, also."

"What would they do to us?"

"*Yo no se*, I don't know," he answers. "Perhaps nothing, perhaps everything."

"How many?"

"Five *soldados* and four Cherokee. *Nueve*. Too many for us to handle."

For the briefest moment I stare at my Spanish amigo, wondering what he's thinking.

"Enrique," I whisper. "Do you wish to join them?"

He shakes his head.

"...No, *ellos no son de mi clase. Son desertores*. They'd just as soon kill as not." He stares at me. "And you they would rape."

I shudder and draw back closer to Akaiyan. For I no longer look like a boy. My hair has grown, and the brown dye faded back to blond.

"Let's go away. Can we backtrack and go around them?"

"We'll wait here," Towaye says then. "For *oosottoo*."

And so we wait for night to fall. Diablo grazes, still wearing the blindfold. I try to sleep but it's impossible, knowing the danger which lies just ahead. Towaye and Akaiyan keep watch, alert for any noise. I can picture in my mind the exchange going on; the Spaniards arguing loudly, bartering beads and trinkets for Cherokee knives and bows. Just who are these renegades, these deserters, as Enrique calls them? Did they run away from a garrison, tracking deep into the southlands to escape Spanish justice? And what might they have done to deserve punishment? Did they come upon an *unqua* gathering, to rape and pillage? Did they steal from their *capitán*, sneaking food from the storage hut? Were they insolent and insubordinate to his authority? All of these questions race through my mind.

I wonder about the Cherokee also. What will they learn about the white man if they deal only with these *soldados*? Will they ever know there are men who don't plunder or rape, who want only to live in peace and harmony with their *unqua* friends?

I'm perplexed and weighted down by the pictures flashing through my mind. I lean against Akaiyan, feeling his strength, knowing his love of all creatures and his respect for nature. Surely mankind is an enigma made, on the one hand, in the image of our true God, acting, on the other, like the devil himself. How can one look upon a man and judge who he is? Only Our Lord and Savior knows the answer, only He can plumb the depths of a man's soul.

By nightfall, all is quiet. Towaye, who's been watching from the woods, comes back to tell us that the *soldados* have gone, heading west and away from our direction. The Cherokee have gone south, leaving just before dusk, running along the stream which is off a half-mile to our left. So the way is once more clear.

We get up quietly, Enrique leading Diablo, keeping the blindfold on so the great *caballo* will move quietly. Towaye leads the way, scouting to the right, to the left, signaling us to move only when he gives the word. We step carefully, trying not to make a sound, still not certain that others might not be waiting in the darkness beyond. Just one more step and we could find ourselves in the midst of the enemy, Spanish or hostile, does it really matter? All that I care about is getting home, back to Croatoan Island, back to my beloved Mother and Father, to Manteo and his people, my people. I look up at the night sky, the stars twinkling and whisper a silent prayer, for Eleanor and her brave group of adventurers, seeking their hearts' dream; and a prayer for me and Akaiyan, so we might reach the fulfillment of ours.

Chapter 10

Enrique's Plan

THERE ARE MORE Spanish soldiers up ahead. Last night, when we hid from the renegades and the Cherokee in their drinking and arguing, we thought it an isolated incident. Now, it seems, we have encountered yet another group of *soldados* on the move. This time they bring their *caballos* with them, and they're fully armed with muskets.

Towaye spots them long before we would have crossed their path. They are hunting, he says, for the deserters from their troop, those very brigands we overheard last evening, carousing, bellowing, bartering with the Cherokee for weapons and silver. There are four, each one leading a fine *caballo*. Upon Enrique's direction, Akaiyan leads Diablo far away, at least a half mile, for if the great black stallion heard his own kind, he'd surely whinny a greeting and give us away. We crouch low in the brush as they pass several yards in front of us.

Three of them are mere privates, it appears, but one is a

capitán by his uniform. He reminds me of Pedro de Avilés though, of course, that one is long dead back at Chesapeake. He speaks in the same domineering voice, ordering his subordinates around in a commanding tone. All of them have a wicked look, which bodes no good for the deserters should they be found.

With Towaye to my left, and Enrique to my right, I should feel secure enough, hidden by thick brambles and bushes. But I find myself trembling still at the sight of such arrogant invaders. I place a hand on Enrique's arm and notice that he's trembling also. Is it my hand or his arm which shakes?

Enrique signals me with his eyes. He nods his head at *los caballos* led behind each man. One is a stallion, five are mares, for there are extra horses who carry many packs. I can read his mind. What a fine addition to our two remaining horses; what a wonderful way to increase and build up our herd. But how could we get them from the *soldados*? And then, to my amazement, Enrique stands and moves out into the open. He holds his hands above his head like a prisoner, moving slowly into the clearing and away from Towaye and me. He's gone crazy, I think.

Towaye gives a low grunt, but remains still. No doubt, he's wondering also, what is this *loco hombre* doing? My body is tensed to run, should they spot us. But their eyes are only for Enrique, and their mouths have dropped open in shock.

"*¿Tráelo aquí?*" asks the *capitán*, immediately turning the reins of his *caballo* over to his subordinate. He pulls a fire arm and points it at Enrique. The other *soldados* begin to talk but are silenced by his look. I hear Enrique speak to them in perfect Spanish, while understanding every word.

"I know you think I look strange, dressed in this costume, but I am unarmed and alone. I've escaped from a group of

hostile Cherokee, far different from their peace-loving brethren, who held me prisoner for several weeks. They stripped me of my uniform and forced me to wear this... this animal skin. I was lucky to hold onto my boots. *Yo estoy solo y gracias a Jesús Cristo por verte.* Now I can rejoin my regiment and gain back *mi honor.*"

The *capitán* is suspicious. He confers with his men, all the while pointing the loaded pistol at Enrique.

"How did you get captured?"

"My regiment hails from the garrison at Chesapeake, far from here. A few of us were on special maneuvers, deep inland. *Mi capitán*, Pedro de Avilés, was killed in ambush. We tracked the Savages for many days and nights, heading south for miles until we were lost. The hostiles surrounded us and killed *mis compañeros.* They kept me alive, though I don't know why."

"You look like *un indio*," grunts one of the *soldados*.

"Only give me a spare uniform, so I can take off these damn skins."

"I've heard of this Pedro de Avilés. He was killed by Savages."

"Yes, yes," says Enrique eagerly. "He is the one, *mi capitán. El era un hombre bueno*, a good man. We sought to avenge his death and see where it has led me!"

The *capitán* hesitates, still pointing his weapon at Enrique. Then he gradually lowers his gun. The others move forward and gather around Enrique, clapping him on the back. One offers him a drink of whiskey from a bottle. Enrique is surrounded.

Towaye grunts and pulls me back deeper into the brush. He whispers that Enrique is a traitor, a *katichlei.*

"*Tnotsaurauweek*," I say, "leave him alone. He knows

what he's doing. He's after the *a hots*."

"Aahh," Towaye nods his head. "*Oosottoo....*" He pulls out his *oosocke nauh*. "We will wait. Then I will help him."

We retreat further, running then full speed to where Akaiyan is waiting with Diablo. Quickly I tell him what's happened. His eyes gleam at the mention of the other *a hots*.

"Where will they camp?"

"The stream is close and dusk approaches. We'll head back when it's dark."

Waiting is the hardest part, wondering if Enrique is all right, wondering how they'll get the *a hots* away from the Spanish. When at last Towaye thinks the time is right, he signals Akaiyan and they slip quietly into the night, while Diablo and I wait. The black is tethered and I pace up and down, wondering what's happening. Akaiyan refuses to let me go with Towaye and him, though I pout mightily. Afterwards, in thinking about it, I'm glad not to be a part of what I know is going to happen. Hours pass. I'm deep in thought and saying many prayers for their safe return, when I hear noises coming through the brush. I crouch low in the grass, my heart beating, beating until my chest will surely burst.

Chapter 11

Horse Thieves

I'M READY TO SPRING upon Diablo's back and race away, if the noises coming through the brush are *soldados*. But then I see Akaiyan and Enrique, with Towaye and five of the six *caballos*. Enrique rides the bay stallion, Akaiyan is on one of the mares, and Towaye on another. The last two mares, carrying the packs, are tethered by *utsera* to Towaye's horse. All of them are exhausted. Akaiyan has a fearsome wound on his arm and Enrique's eye is swollen shut. Only Towaye looks unharmed.

"What happened. Tell me quickly."

They dismount only to make sure no one is following. Then Akaiyan mounts Diablo and I'm given his mare. Without talking, we move quickly through the darkness away from the encounter, heading north once more.

We ride for several hours, the only sound the thud of the *a hots'* hooves. The moon sails between thick clouds, our way guided by shadows. Many times I think I see *soldados* lurking in the bushes, behind the trees, but it's only the silvery light playing tricks. Diablo's ears are laced back. He smells the intruder stallion and is clearly agitated. Akaiyan is once again having a hard time controlling him. The bay, too, is unused to his new rider; he bucks and kicks out several times, snorting in anger. It's clear to me that we'll have to keep these two stallions separated.

On we ride. At one point I can see Akaiyan's arm. The blood is still oozing from his wound, trickling down. I rein my mare in and call to him,

"Akaiyan, I must see to your arm."

I bind the wound with strips of deerskin torn from my clothing. There's not much I can do here, without clean water to wash it, without *auoona hau*, moss, to keep infection away. Though the cut is deep, it's missed the bone and arteries. With care, it should heal properly.

We continue to ride until all of us, human and *a hots*, are exhausted. We pull the animals up and dismount, sinking thankfully to the forest floor, there to rest. Akaiyan's arm is sore, and the bandage slightly reddened, but it appears to have stopped any further bleeding. Enrique's eye is now almost completely shut, swollen and beginning to turn purple. Towaye is unharmed and sees to the *a hots*, keeping the two stallions tethered securely at far distances from each other. Somewhere there must be a stream running, for he leads the mares to water, then comes back for each stallion separately. I can see how good he's becoming with the *a hots*. Like all the *unqua*, he seems to have a natural talent for communicating with each animal, whispering to it in *unqua* words, able to read its mind and foresee its needs.

"What happened?" I ask then, as we catch our breath.

"*Fue magnífico,*" Enrique replies. "We waited until they

were all asleep, except the one on guard. Towaye crept up behind him and *silencio, él ya no fue un problema.* Then Akaiyan and I crept upon each one sleeping...."

He doesn't finish, nor do I ask. I can picture easily the scenario; the sleeping men awakening in a daze, a knife thrust, the end to a life. Part of me is exhilarated hearing about our victory; another part is saddened that violence has become a way of life for my *unqua* friends. As if reading my mind, Akaiyan whispers,

"We knew of killing long before you came. Sometimes it was necessary to protect our homes and families from marauding tribes. We prefer not to take a life but will, if needed."

"One escaped," Towaye says then. "I chased him into the woods but I was on foot, and he had a head start."

"Will he follow us?"

Enrique smiles.

"I doubt it. He was headed in the opposite direction *tan rápido como podía correr su caballo.*"

"The bay is *magnífico*," I smile at Enrique. "He and the mares will increase our herd."

"He's a difficult animal, equal to Diablo in strength. We must not allow them to get close, or they'll fight."

"I'll give him a name. Let's see, I'll call him *Auhuntwaar*, Thunderer."

"*Es un buen nombre*," Enrique nods his head. "One of the mares is pregnant already, probably by him."

"How do you know?"

He smiles again.

"See her swollen belly. She is well rounded. Another two months and you'll have *un nuevo potrico* to play with."

"We're horse thieves," I say then, feeling very guilty. "We stole horses that didn't belong to us, just like we did at the Spanish garrison."

Enrique shrugs his shoulders.

"We'll treat them *mucho mejor* than their owners did. See the whip marks on the bay's withers? See the spur scars on the mares' sides? I don't feel bad taking them. I've seen how the *unqua* love *los caballos. Estaran mas felices con nosotros.*"

I squeeze his hand and throw my arms about him.

"You're like a brother to me."

"*Y tú, mi bella Jess, eres como otra querida hermana.*"

Akaiyan pulls me over to where he's sitting, staring at me with his deep brown eyes.

"You like him?"

"He's my *caunotka*, brother."

"And you will be my *kateocca* when we return?"

I kiss him quickly on the lips, smoothing away his doubt.

"I want to be your *kateocca* very much, when we return."

Chapter 12

The Stallions

ON THE LONG RIDE northeast, we see isolated hunting and foraging parties. Some are Cherokee; others belong to the Keyauwee and Catawba tribes who range far and wide, and even the fierce warlike Neusiok. But no matter, they all look up when they hear our thunder hooves, then scatter in great alarm at the monsters charging down upon them. Few have seen *a hots* before, and many stories will be told around tribal fires late at night, about the demons from *popogusso* who ride out of the mists, part Indian, part animal! Akaiyan and Enrique have taken to giving war-whoops whenever we see them, adding effectively to their fright.

The mares are all fine animals, three brown, one chestnut with white foot markings, and one bay stallion, whose hide shines like embers in a dying fire. I wonder what Manteo will say when he sees us riding up from the beach at Croatoan, with two great stallions and four mares. I know how pleased he is by the *a hots* we brought him from Chesapeake, Beauty and her foal, Star, and Diablo. His eyes will gleam with delight. And Father and Mother, they'll be happy too, to see their daughter returning safely.

Akaiyan's arm has grown infected. The flesh is puffy around the wound, and streaks of yellow and red are forming. Towaye says we must lance the wound and let the evil drain out. So that afternoon, we pull up the horses near a stream, tether them and examine the packs upon the last mare. We find hidden caches of food, ropes and knives, maps, blankets and silver and gold coins. And wonder of wonders, some medicinal powders. Towaye smells each powder and tastes it carefully with his tongue. Some he spits out; with others he nods his head and stores them away for future use.

I can see now why the Spanish have been so successful in their explorations of this wilderness world. They came much better prepared than our English colonists, with more supplies, better maps and their *caballos*. The horses carry them far and wide; they're able to bring more supplies on each journey; they can more easily escape their enemies on horse-back. And, it seems, their passion for gold and silver drives them onward, not the willingness to settle in one place and raise a family. I run my fingers through the silver and gold coins. To the *unqua* they mean nothing; to Enrique, they might buy his passage home, should he wish to go.

We carefully wash Akaiyan's festering wound. Then Towaye takes his *oosocke nauh* and makes a long cut down the length of the wound. Akaiyan grits his teeth against the pain, while he crushes the bones of my hand as he holds on. Not a sound escapes his lips. The wound runs yellow pus and smells badly, but when at last it's clear of putrefaction, Towaye cleans it again and sprinkles some yellow powder taken from the Spanish. We bind it with a fresh strip of buckskin. Akaiyan's brown skin gleams white against the pain; beads of sweat cover his face. But he springs to his feet, thanks Towaye and we mount up again.

It's not long after that the two stallions almost get into a fight. Enrique explains that one of the mares is reaching her season for mating. The bay circles her constantly, nipping at her ears, wanting to mount her. Diablo smells her too, and wants her equally. At first, I laugh to see them, each one in a courtship dance of sorts.

"Will you marry me?" I say with a smile as Diablo extends his long neck forward to touch her nose.

"No, me," I speak for the bay, as he paws the ground at the end of his tether.

"There'll be trouble," Enrique warns and almost as he says that, Thunderer snaps the *utsera* which holds him to the tree and lays back his ears to charge Diablo.

"Whoa," calls Enrique, trying to grab the rope as it trails past. He misses and goes down. The bay rumbles past him, then rears and strikes out at Diablo. All the mares are snorting in terror. Towaye isn't certain what to do, never having seen two stallions in a battle. But Enrique lunges at the trailing *utsera* and finally grabs it.

"*¡Apúrate!* help me," he cries to Akaiyan and Towaye. All three of them pull on the rope and, though they're dragged several feet by his strength, manage to stop the bay stallion and pull him over to another tree. There, Towaye tethers him with a new *utsera*, one much stronger this time.

"What would have happened?" I ask Enrique.

"*Puede ser que se hayan matado*, they might have killed each other," he answers. "Certainly, one would have been seriously *dañado*. I will take the mare and Thunderer far away, where he can pleasure her and himself. By the time I come back, she will know motherhood in about eleven months and the bay will be quiet, *te prometo*."

I watch as he and Towaye lead the bay stallion and the mare away. Diablo quiets down, though the whites of his eyes show for several moments. The other *a hots* calm down also, and I'm able to relax, snuggling in a moment of aloneness with Akaiyan.

"Will you marry me?" I ask with a smile on my face. For a moment he doesn't understand, then he smiles back.

"I am a fierce stallion who longs for you," he says with urgency. "I could take you just like the bay."

"After a proper marriage," I remind him.

"It is almost impossible to wait," he replies, smothering me fiercely in kisses.

Chapter 13

Neusiok Danger

WE'VE REACHED CLOSE to the mainland where Roanoak Island lies opposite. The ride home has been swifter upon the *a hots'* backs. Keeping the powerful bay and black stallions separated has been more difficult. Enrique was right about the bay. After he mated with the mare in season, he was much more docile. Before that, we could hear him through the trees, neighing in his glory and the mare calling loudly to him. This made Diablo frantic.

It was all Akaiyan could do to hold Diablo, even though he was tethered. The black's ears were back, his eyes rolled white and he kept side-stepping and rearing. When at last, all was quiet in the woodlands, Diablo calmed down and let himself be led further away. When Enrique and Towaye brought the love-sick pair back, Diablo was off by himself munching on new sweet grass.

"*Es un buen caballo macho,*" Enrique nods at the bay. "He has just made a beautiful babe."

I smile. The mare seems contented enough, concentrating now on grazing. The bay allows me to touch his sweaty sides and scratch behind his ears.

"Well, *gran caballo*," I murmur, "love is a powerful thing," thinking of Akaiyan and me. The strange stirrings I feel whenever Akaiyan and I kiss, or when he holds me closely, must be akin to what the stallion and mare have felt.

"It is nature's way of reproducing the species," Enrique comments, watching my face. "I see that same look on Akaiyan's face whenever he stares at you."

I blush most profusely. Enrique throws back his head and laughs.

"And I had the same look with my beloved one back *en España*...." He grows sad. "But she couldn't wait for me to return. *He oído que ella tiene un niño ahora, y esperando otro,* I heard she has a child now, with yet another on the way."

"You get more news from Spain than we get from England," I say. "Do you know what's happened? Has Philip won against Elizabeth?"

Enrique grows most thoughtful.

"We last heard that Philip and the Armada have lost against your English ships. But smaller battles still are waged, here and there, among the pirates and privateers who haven't heard. They're after any English ship they can catch." He pauses. "Wars die hard and *soldados* like to fight them."

"That means John White will soon be returning here," I cry excitedly. "I must hasten home to tell Father and Mother that the war is over."

"*Nosotros tenemos nuestros propios problemas aquí,* we have our own troubles here," Enrique says then grimly, and I look to where he's staring. A group of hostiles have stepped through the woods, appearing almost magically, and are

52

standing in front of us, bows ready, arrows drawn and aimed right at us.

I want to call out to Akaiyan, hidden with Diablo deeper in the trees, but Towaye places a warning hand on my arm.

"Neusiok," he whispers, "warriors...."

The Savages have painted stripes down their cheeks. They speak an *unqua* dialect I haven't heard before. They stare at the horses, grazing behind us, barely able to take their eyes off them. The leader, a fearsome sort, speaks rapidly to his comrades. He signals them to approach the *a hots*, at the same time motioning us over to one side. Towaye raises his hand in greeting.

Towaye then delivers words in that same strange dialect. I can't understand a thing he's saying, but the Neusiok seem to. They nod their heads and confer excitedly with each other. One of them, a younger brave about Akaiyan's age, goes over to the bay stallion and reaches out his hand. The bay rears and snorts, stamping his hooves and making earth fly. The Neusiok backs hurridly away.

Towaye continues talking to them. I wonder how Manteo's shaman knows this strange dialect so well. Towaye holds both hands outstretched. He seems to be making an offer. Enrique and I are frozen where we stand.

The leader nods his head and Towaye goes to one of the pack mares. He reaches into one bundle and pulls out the gold and silver coins of the Spanish. I want to cry out, 'No, that will buy Enrique's passage home,' but don't dare. Towaye offers the leader the full pouch of coins, unties one *a hots* and leads her over to him. The Neusiok back away when he approaches with the mare. She is one which isn't pregnant and I'm glad, for I know Towaye is offering her to them, along with the coins. They talk rapidly between them and suddenly, the bows and arrows are lowered and I find myself breathing in great gulps of air.

The Neusiok disappear as rapidly as they came, one minute there, the next blending into the woodlands like magic.

"The danger is over," Towaye tells me in Croatoan, while I stare with new-found admiration at this man of magic, this shaman of whom I was once terribly afraid. We wait for several moments, then Towaye gives a low birdlike call. Several more moments, and Akaiyan appears by my side leading a blindfolded Diablo. Poor *a hots*, I think with a sigh of relief, he seems to spend most of his life with a blindfold over his eyes.

"We must hurry," Towaye says then, "for while they seem content with the coins and the one, they may decide they want them all."

So we quickly mount up and gallop east, toward Roanoak, toward our beautiful homeland, minus one brown *a hots* and some Spanish coins. A fair trade for our lives!

Chapter 14

Back Home Again

WHAT A SIGHT we must be, riding up from the beach at Croatoan. And what a long journey! We swim the *a hots* across from the mainland to Roanoak, letting the two pregnant mares ride the raft which Akaiyan found from where they'd hidden it. The two stallions swim strongly, pulling the third mare by their sheer brute strength. Enrique and I paddle the *ooshun-nawa*, while Towaye and Akaiyan handle the mares. Even so, it's a long and dangerous trip across the waters. By the time we reach Roanoak, the animals are exhausted. We rest there and then make our way across to the far shore. This time even the pregnant mares have to swim, but it's a much shorter span. Once upon the outer banks, we celebrate and allow ourselves to enjoy a much-needed sleep.

It takes less time to ride down from Roanoak since we're all on horseback. Once again, we wait for the tide to be at ebb, then swim them all across. The pregnant mare, whom I've named "Ottea," Fawn, heaves and blows most heartily. Her time to foal is approaching, and I think Enrique is mistaken when he gives her two more months. She looks exactly the way Beauty looked right before she gave birth to Star. I only hope this long and arduous trip won't cause her to go into labor too early.

It's early morn when we mount the *a hots* and walk them slowly up the embankment toward the trees. I want to gallop all the way to our village, but pity lets me spare the exhausted animals. In actuality, I can take the time to enjoy the loveliness of this island; the trees are almost in full bloom, the flowers just unfurling their petals to the sun. It's May and we're home at last.

Manteo's eyes almost spring from his head when he sees our entourage: Enrique, Akaiyan, Towaye and me, and *cinco caballos*. The two stallions are too exhausted to nip at each other, or rear and paw the empty air. The mares' heads droop down. I promise them lots of rest and good food when we dismount. But it's Enrique who sees to all of them, first taking the mares to the sheltering house where he tethers and feeds them, then separating the stallions into two different areas.

"Tomorrow," he says, "we must build enclosures around each stallion so they can run free and never meet each other."

Manteo looks at Akaiyan's arm, still healing, and then puts his arm about his shoulder.

"My son, it is good to see you. You must tell me about your journey."

He stares at Enrique, leading the horses to shelter.

"I have never seen so many *a hots*."

"The two mares are pregnant," I say excitedly. "One will give birth very soon."

Manteo leaves us then and goes to examine the stallions. Diablo, who's used to the *unqua*, lowers his head to let the great chief scratch behind his ears. Thunderer snorts and frets when Manteo approaches.

"It will take time," I translate for Enrique, who gathers grain for them. I step back to view this scene: the Spanish *soldado* and the Indian chief, both of them admiring our new-found treasure. For surely *a hots*, to the *unqua*, are like gold to the Spaniards, wealth beyond measure.

I turn and go to see dear Mother and Father.

"I thought you'd never return," Mother cries, sobbing on my shoulder. "God has surely bestowed His blessings upon you, Jess, to bring you home safe and sound to us."

"I missed you so," I whisper, hugging her. "And you, too," I say to Thomas. How tall he's grown, filling out in shoulders and chest. How soon to be a man!

"And how's Father?"

To my great alarm, Mother breaks anew into fresh weeping. She sobs without end.

"She's been so brave," Wenefrid Powell says, coming over. "For your dear father is sicker than before."

I want to run and see him, but Mother cautions me.

"Say nothing. Show no alarm on your face. I fear his days are numbered."

It's with great trepidation that I enter our lodge house, to see dear Father and kiss him gently on the cheek. He's so weak that he can't even rise from the bed without holding a hand to his chest.

"My dearest Jess," he murmurs, coughing over and over. "I've said many prayers to Our Good Lord for your safe return."

"God surely watched over me, Father," I reply, keeping my look light and smiling. "For my greatest reward is to see you again. We'll get you better, don't worry."

He coughs. "Not this time, Jess. I fear the ague has its grip on me and won't let go. It hurts every time I cough."

I see again the blood flecking his lips. He wipes it away with a cloth.

"I tried to keep this from your dear Mother, but she saw the blood-stained rags. She's been sick with worry over me, over you. Thank God she doesn't have to worry about you any more."

"I love you, Father," I whisper, holding tightly onto his hand. It's like holding the hand of an old man. The strong grip of my father is gone. I lean my head against his shoulder, remembering how he used to hold me on his knee, remembering his strength, his power, and the tears run silently down my cheeks.

Chapter 15

The A Hots

DURING THIS TIME of joy and sorrow, I'm so confused. The joy springs from my delight at being home once again. My sorrows are two-fold, the loss of Eleanor and little Virginia, and the despair at seeing my father so gravely ill. For deep in my heart, I know Mother is right; his days are, indeed, numbered.

How can this happen to a man once so strong? One moment well; the next, languishing in bed, weak, coughing up blood. I can remember how my father hewed timber and lifted beams to build houses. Those days are gone forever.

I see my mother walking around as if in a daze, carrying his illness heavy upon her shoulders. How I wish there is a magic potion to give him, some cure which will cease his coughing and heal his damaged lungs. Where is God, who turns His back on my prayers? Has He forsaken me, after watching out so long for my well-being? Does He not love my father? These are questions for which I've no answers.

I turn in my anguish to the *a hots*, those gentle creatures who carried us so patiently on their backs through the dangers of the wilderness, back to this safe haven. I'm enthralled by them. I love their deep brown eyes, their soft velvet noses, the way they push against me for affection, or whicker softly when they see me coming. I don't even mind grooming them, or cleaning out their stalls. I gladly fetch them water, alongside Enrique or Akaiyan or Quayah, his younger brother.

Star greets me in sweet remembrance, pushing herself against me. She bobs her head up and down and pretends to run away when I call, only to look back and then come trotting over. Beauty is as gentle as ever, tossing her head and walking over when she sees me. I miss Little Swan, but Fawn is just as sweet, quite round in the fullness of her pregnancy. Enrique tells me that I was right after all, she is closer to birthing than he'd first thought. The other newly-pregnant mare I've named "Chaunoctay," Little Otter. The last mare is a chestnut, the brilliant color of the sun, so I've named her "Qui-hei-ratse," Sunlight, in honor of that golden orb from which all life comes.

Diablo looks for food when I come near, trying to nibble my fingers. I scratch behind his ears and he stands contented with his head lowered. Enrique and some of the *unqua* have built a fenced enclosure for him, where he can run freely. Across the way and separated by the *a hots'* shelter, Thunderer roams his own fenced paddock. He is a big bay stallion, slightly larger than Diablo. He doesn't come to me when I call his name, but I know he will eventually. I have lots of time and patience.

We're rewarded in our admiration of the horses when Fawn goes into labor. Like Beauty, one early morn she sinks to the ground groaning, her sides glistening sweat. Enrique has stayed with her all night.

"She'll give birth before long," he tells me and Akaiyan. This time, Manteo comes to watch, and several of the *unqua*. They stand back so as not to alarm her. Only Enrique is close by, soothing and comforting her the way he did with Beauty. And like the *bella yegua*, she has an easy birth, the foal slipping out with no trouble. It's a boy foal, a colt, Enrique says, with long spindly legs. It staggers to its feet and Fawn licks it dry. I turn to see Manteo smiling broadly. He raises his hands to the dawn's light and calls out his prayer.

"Oh, Great Spirit, mighty and all-seeing. We thank you for this gift of the *a hots* and especially, this new life. This *a hots* shall grow to be big and strong, fast as the wind. In honor of the wind spirit, I shall name him *Hoonoch ou-cuhnnahar*, Swift as the Wind."

He comes close and blesses the colt with his hands. Fawn looks anxious, but then lets him stroke her. He plucks a feather from his hair and weaves it so swiftly into her mane that she doesn't even notice.

"This *oosnooqua* is our bond, mother, for your gift of life to the *unqua*. From now on, *ka chu-techne kichta unquahah*, you are one with the *unqua*."

Then he turns and strides quickly away, leaving me in awe.

Akaiyan squeezes my hand.

"My father is pleased with the *a hots*. One day he will ride Hoonoch far and wide."

Quayah hangs around, doing what Enrique bids him. Akaiyan smiles at his younger brother.

"Soon you will ride as well as Enrique. Soon all the *unqua* shall ride as fast as the wind. See how fortune smiles upon us."

He sweeps his arm to encompass the *a hots*, all eight of them. Then he turns to me and takes my hand.

"Come, it is time to ask my father's blessing upon our joining. It is time to seek your parents' favor."

Chapter 16

An Indian Wedding

I'M ALONE with Father in our lodge house. Mother is with Mistress Steueens, taking a much-needed break. I've promised to stay with him, making sure he sips his hot honey tea, while reading some of his favorite passages from the Holy Bible.

"The thing that hast been, shalt be; and that which is done shalt be done: for there be no new thing under the sun."

"I always liked Ecclesiastes," he says. "Read me something else."

"To every thing there is a season," I read on, "a time to every purpose under heaven: a time in which we are born, and a time to die...."

"Tell me about the new foal."

"He's wonderful, Father, full of life and spirit. Manteo has blessed him and named him *Hoonoch ou-cuhnnahar*."

"What does that mean?"

"He'll run swift as the wind."

"Aah," he says, leaning back and smiling. "I like that."

He coughs again and stares at me long and hard,

"For many are called but few be chosen. Who said that?"

"Why, Our Lord and Savior Himself, Jesus Christ."

"I think you're chosen, dear Jess, to carry our word and spirit to the *unqua*, perhaps to live among them and teach them...."

"...and learn from them, too, Father."

"Indeed, perhaps to learn from them, too."

He begins to cough anew.

"Ah, this wretched affliction shall be the death of me.... It's your mother who's so opposed to this union. As for me, I only wish to see you happy. Your heart is well-known to me, dearest daughter."

"I love him truly, Father."

He sighs.

"Yes, I know. You must persuade your mother. And that," he laughs, immediately coughing again, "will be your biggest challenge."

She cries softly, her shoulders sagging.

"I knew this was coming. I've been dreading this day...."

"...but...."

"Hush, hush, who am I to say where or with whom your happiness lies. I've had mine, Our Good Lord knows, soon to lose it, I'm afraid."

"Oh, Mother."

"Have you spoken with your father?"

"He says that you're my biggest challenge."

She smiles.

"Indeed, I think your biggest challenge is yet to come." She holds out her arms to me. "Come and give me a hug, while I... give you my blessing, for I can see the fire which burns so hotly within you."

And so the time comes when I stand side by side with Akaiyan in front of Manteo, Sinopa and the rest of the *unqua*. Mother, Thomas and Father, too, are there, for he's insisted on giving me away. Master and Mistress Steueens, Wenefrid Powell, her husband and babe, and all our good English folk remaining have willingly joined the ceremony to see me wed with Akaiyan, my chosen, my beloved one.

It's a short, uncomplicated ceremony, full of sweet ritual. Mother surprises me by unwrapping a dress of white which she has kept all this time unknown to me, traveling from England, to Roanoak, to Croatoan Island. The *unqua* women have woven flowers to wear as a wreath in my hair. I have Akaiyan's amulet as a necklace. I've asked Thomas to read a passage from our Holy Bible, my favorite passage from the Book of Ruth:

"For whither thou goest, I will go; and where
thou dwellest, there I will dwell: thy people are
my people, and thy God is my God."

I hear Mother's sob catch in her throat and turn, for the briefest moment, to smile at her. She stares at me then gently nods her head. I wish at that moment that sweet Eleanor was standing there also, sharing my happiness.

Manteo and Sinopa offer their prayers to the Great Spirit for our happiness and good fortune. The *unqua* wish us to have many children, for children are a blessing for all people.

"*Its warke tewots woccanookne,*" smiles Sinopa.

Father, who has leaned heavily on Mother up to now, walks slowly forward and takes my hand, placing it in Akaiyan's. He leans down and kisses my cheek, then nods to Akaiyan. I can hear Mother's soft crying.

Sinopa wraps ribbons of flowers around our wrists, bind-ing us for all time. She says a special *unqua* prayer, then smiles and nods her head. Akaiyan leans down and kisses me, a gentle kiss upon my lips. Mistresses Steueens and Powell give cries of joy. I see Mother wiping her eyes furiously with a handkerchief then she, too, manages a faint smile.

There's much celebration after, with songs and dances, both *unqua* and *nickreruroh*. A feast is served and the children play games. Then in late afternoon, when the sun is beginning to streak the sky with gold, after hours of merriment and laughter, Akaiyan takes my hand and leads me to my parents. I kiss both Mother and Father on the cheek, say a quiet goodbye, and follow my husband to the lodge house built especially for us at the far end of the village. There, alone at last with Akaiyan, we share our first embrace as man and wife. He kisses me joyously and I, in turn, kiss him with equal passion. As the laughter and singing fade in the background, we sweetly begin our new life together.

Chapter 17

Star Escapes

WE'RE AWAKENED in the morning, not by singing birds, but by loud cries. We both jump up and pull aside the covering which shields our privacy. The *unqua* are running to and fro; I can see Enrique waving his arms frantically and watch, in horror, to see little Star trotting off in the distance, into the woods surrounding our village.

"Star's escaped," Enrique says to us as we run up.

"How did it happen?"

"Something frightened her, I think," pants Enrique, for he's out of breath from running. "We'll have to catch her and bring her back safely."

We run to the *a hots*. Beauty is calling out frantically and the other mares are jostling each other. Diablo is snorting and from his paddock, Thunderer is pawing the ground.

"Take Beauty," Enrique says, "for without her, we've no chance of getting Star."

We spur the horses on toward the trees. By now, Mother

67

has run out of her house, and the *unqua* are frantically telling her, gestures and all, what's happened.

"Be careful," she calls to me as we go galloping by.

A little filly can go fast when she's frightened. Through the trees we can see glimpses of her bobbing tail, but she weaves in and out and disappears from sight.

"There's something chasing her," Akaiyan cries to us in the lead. "Head her toward the beach."

We maneuver the horses through the thick growth of trees until, at last, they start to thin. We're approaching the sand dunes of the far beach. I can only hope Star won't plunge into the water in her fright.

We pull up the *a hots* to see her racing back and forth upon the beach, the sand flying in all directions. Then we see what's been chasing her. A *squarrena*, thin and hungry, paces warily in the sand behind her. She kicks out at it in panic, but it crouches, ready to spring.

"*Un loco*," Enrique calls, "surely crazy, for why else would it follow her this far?"

"It must be very hungry," I whisper, feeling both sorry for the wolf and afraid for Star.

"It's a female with cubs, no doubt," says Akaiyan. "My Uttewiraratse looked like an easy target."

I translate for Enrique, who curses suddenly under his breath.

"Damn, I forgot my musket."

But I see then that Akaiyan hasn't forgotten his bow and arrow. He quickly dismounts, flings the reins to Enrique and sprints to within shooting range. The female wolf spots him coming but won't give up her stalk. She turns to snarl at Akaiyan, then continues after Star who, by now, is exhausted and frantic with fear. Just when the wolf is about to spring,

Akaiyan's arrow finds its mark. There's a short yelp of pain, and the *squarrena* falls over on her side, the arrow protruding from her chest.

"This isn't a good wedding present," I say sadly, walking up to see the she-wolf close her eyes and die. Akaiyan has reached Star and managed to grab her. Feeling his soothing hands, she lets herself be led back to us, where Enrique tethers her to Beauty. The *bella yegua* sniffs her all over, then licks her reassuringly.

"This female has cubs," comments Akaiyan, examining the wolf. Sure enough, it's easy to see how swollen she is from nursing pups.

"There must be a den somewhere in the trees," Akaiyan continues. "We'll have to find them."

"Why?"

"If we do not, the pups will die of starvation."

"What will we do when we find them?" I ask.

"We will have to kill them ourselves. Better to die a swift death than slowly of hunger."

He picks up the wolf's body and walks toward the woodlands.

"I will bury her," he says, "for her pelt is no good to us and the scavengers should not get her."

I follow sadly. How hungry must that poor wolf have been to brave the Indian village, coming right into its midst to seek food? But how glad I am that she didn't kill Star. I let Enrique take the *a hots*, along with Star, back toward our village. I'll stay with Akaiyan and help him find the den. He digs a hole and buries the wolf mother. Then he says an *unqua* prayer to set her spirit free for its final journey. After that, we backtrack for several miles, winding in and out the trees, looking for signs of a den. But we can't seem to find any. At one point,

Akaiyan throws down his bow and arrows, holds out his arms, and I go to him.

"I did not think to spend my wedding day searching for *squarrena*," he says, kissing me.

"Nor I," I reply, sinking to the earthy floor as he touches me, my body like fire wherever he moves his hands. The world around us fades, the birds, the insects' humming, the early sunlight winking through the trees. All is Akaiyan, his mouth, his warmth, his sweetness, and nature embraces us with her love.

Chapter 18

The Wolf Cubs

I LIE IN AKAIYAN'S ARMS, listening to the music of the world around us. Then I hear the soft mewling sounds, like kittens newborn. I sit up abruptly.

"Listen," I put a finger to my lips. "Can't you hear that?"

Akaiyan jumps to his feet, pulling me with him. We both strain to hear.

"Over here," he whispers and leads me to a large up-rooted tree trunk. The hole underneath is dark and big.

"Be careful," I caution as he bends down and reaches a hand inside. I wait with baited breath. He withdraws his hand and drops something dark and furry down on the ground at my feet. It's a tiny wolf cub, blind and helpless. I crouch down to see it closer.

"Oh, sweet little thing."

Akaiyan reaches in two more times and pulls out two other furry bundles. They squeak with tiny voices, nuzzling each other, nuzzling my hand.

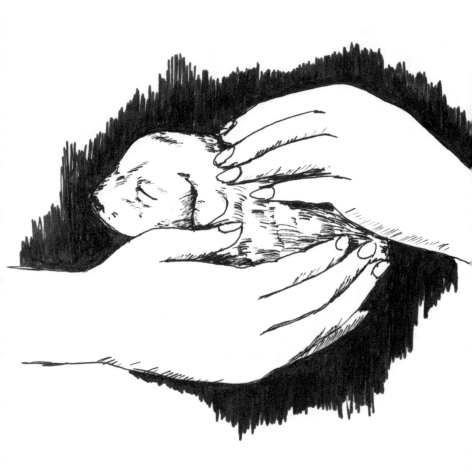

"Any more?"

He reaches under again searching with his hand.

"Nothing. Only these three."

I gently stroke each tiny body, picking each one up in turn and holding it close to my face.

"Oh, they're perfect. So small, so lovely."

"*Squarrena*," Akaiyan frowns. "One day they'll be big enough to hunt, to bring down a deer, to seize a small *unqua* child."

He reaches for a large stone.

"Oh, don't, don't kill them, please."

"They can not live without the mother."

"Can't we take them home, can't we feed them?"

"The *unqua* reveres the *squarrena* from a distance, recognizing his prowess as a hunter. But to bring him to his hearth, his home, would be against the laws of nature."

"Don't you have dogs? The English have dogs as pets."

"*Unqua* have no need of pets."

He stares at me long and hard.

"You are crying," he says finally.

"I can't bear the thought of killing them. They're so helpless. Surely we were meant to find them. The wolf's spirit has asked us to look after her babies."

He laughs out loud.

"She did no such thing!"

"Oh, yes, she did. She led us to this place and made them cry out just so I'd hear them."

Akaiyan is shaking his head, a look of puzzlement on his face.

"What will my father say when he sees these cubs?"

"We'll tell him they're a present from the wolf spirit. Won't he understand?"

And so, Akaiyan and I bring the wolf babies back to our village. Their tiny mouths seek out warm milk and we have none. Their cries grow weaker until, at last, they're asleep, warm against my bodice. I look down at my bulging front and begin to laugh.

"I look funny."

Manteo frowns when he sees what we've brought home from the forest.

"We cannot keep them."

"Oh, but...."

"When they grow big, they will kill our animals."

"Not if we train them."

He shakes his head at me.

"*A hots* are one thing, *squarrena* another. I will not allow it."

Then when he sees my downcast look,

"Little Bird, how will you feed them? How will you train them not to kill?"

Manteo turns and leaves. Akaiyan and I walk over to where the *a hots* are.

"We cannot keep them."

"He didn't say we couldn't. He just asked how we'd feed them."

Akaiyan stares at me.

"I do not understand the English mind. When they grow, how will we stop them from killing?"

"All dogs were once wolves."

He shakes his head.

"My father will not be pleased."

But I set my mouth in a hard line and take out the little bundles of fur. I won't give them up, I won't, for I've seen too much of death and dying. I hold one sleeping pup up to Fawn's

74

nose. She lays back her ears, then sniffs. There's no enemy wolf smell, just cub and my scent from its touching my skin. Fawn gently nibbles its fur.

"We can use Fawn's milk. She has plenty to spare."

He stares incredulously at me.

"A *squarrena* can not suckle a... horse," using the English word.

"Do you have any female goats?"

He shakes his head again.

"None that are suckling young."

"Then we've no choice. We'll take Fawn's milk, just like a cow."

How strange, to reach under the warm belly of an *a hots* and find the swollen source of life. Fawn kicks when I first touch her full teat, gently squeezing it. But she soon quiets down and I'm able to squirt a little milk into a curved shell. I take the first sleepy pup and dip his nose into the warm liquid. He sputters and squeaks a mewling cry. But then, a little pink tongue comes out and he licks his nose. Again and again, I dip his nose, he licks it, until at last he seems satisfied.

I do the same with the other two pups. But the last one is much smaller than the others. He doesn't lick the milk and it drips off his muzzle. I open his mouth and insert a milky finger. He doesn't respond. I hold him to my ear, listening desperately for the faint heartbeat. I can't hear any. The littlest pup is dead.

Somehow this death affects me greatly. I start to weep, great tears rolling down my cheek. I try to blow my warm breath into the little *squarrena's* mouth. I rub his tiny chest. As all seems hopeless, he suddenly sputters and coughs, then a little pink tongue flicks out.

"Oh, Akaiyan," I cry out excitedly, "see, he lives, he lives!"

I'm still crying as I stick my milky finger once again in his mouth. He squirms, then begins to suck.

I feel Akaiyan's hands upon my shoulders, rubbing me gently and I lean back against his warmth, his strength, closing my eyes. The cub sucks on my finger as I dip it again and again in the milk. Oh, thank you, Great Spirit, for your love of all creatures, big and small, even these tiny *squarrena*.

Chapter 19

Thunderstorm

THE WOLF CUBS continue to grow. Last week, their eyes opened and they began to explore where they live. Fawn has totally accepted them, for they smell of her warm sweet milk and I've rubbed them against Hoonoch, her colt. She steps carefully around them as they explore her stall, placing her great hooves with care. I'm amazed that she hasn't injured them. But at night when Hoonoch suckles and is in with her, we move them to a crate Enrique has constructed. There they snuggle and settle down for the night. The animal house echoes with the sounds of babes, both *a hots* and *squarrena*.

Manteo strides about the camp frowning whenever he looks in their direction. But Enrique tells me that on more than one occasion, he's seen Manteo emerging from their house, a faint smile hovering about the corners of his mouth. I know he doesn't approve, yet at the same time is fascinated by the idea of taming them. I've told Akaiyan the story of how dogs were once wild, just like the *squarrena*.

As with *los caballos*, Enrique has taken them under his care, calling them *los lobitos*. Today, we mixed finely-ground oats in with their milk. Their little tongues lapped up the new food eagerly. I've named the largest, Teethha, the next, Che-chou, and my favorite, the littlest, Sooka. Already, they come running when I call out to them.

This pleasure is countered by my dear father's illness. He grows weaker each day. Not even Towaye's medicine can help him. Mother has big black circles under her eyes, from listening to him cough all night, both of them unable to sleep. She hardly cries anymore, her tears "all dried up," she says.

And with the waxing and waning of the summer moon, comes the cessation of my menses. I've not told anyone, not even Akaiyan. When the time is right, when it's just perfect, then I'll share my joy with him. Oh, how I wish sweet Eleanor were here, for I'd gladly tell her. As one woman to another, we'd smile in the sweetness of this fulfillment of life, this mystery from God, bonded with women throughout all history, from Eve's first joy down through the ages. Oh, what rapture it is to be a woman, loving a man, knowing you carry the seed of his love deep within you!

I think often of Eleanor, little Virginia and the others. Have they reached their intended destination yet, finding George and the first group of brave colonists who left us so long ago? I can envision sweet Eleanor scraping and scratching her messages upon each rough stone as she moves further south and deeper inland: "Father - almost there - follow, July 1589."

I wonder if they've avoided dangers or met with wandering groups of Cherokee, possibly friendly, possibly not. I say many prayers for the safe-keeping of my dear friend, almost sister, and her child. I think of little Mistress Payne sitting astride Little Swan, marveling at her new height. I think of Little Swan, growing her babe as I'm now growing mine. I weep in my anxiety that they're safe, protected by Our Lord Jesus Christ, protected by the Great Spirit who watches over us all.

The August thunderstorms whip across Croatoan Island from the south, from the east, carrying the fury of the mighty sea. Rains pelt us almost every other day, tearing at the brush roofs of our houses, washing away the dunes and re-carving new sculptures in them. The sea is mad with whitecaps, the trees bend and sway in the wind's anger. At those times, Enrique sleeps with the *a hots*, bringing them comfort and the sound of his soothing voice. Even Akaiyan leaves our lodge house when the wind and rain are at their height, helping Enrique with all the animals.

Star, especially, is afraid of the lightning and the wind. She rolls her eyes until the whites show, trembling in her fear. Enrique tethers her near to the *bella yegua* and sleeps in their stall. Diablo and Thunderer stir restlessly throughout each storm, as if the gods of the sea are calling to them. Each one lathers his hide until the tempest subsides.

Only Teethha, Che-chou and Sooka don't seem to mind. They cock their little heads to one side whenever the thunderclaps sound, but then continue to romp and play unafraid. I'm terribly worried the *a hots* will trample them as they fret and sidestep in their stalls. But the three *squarrena* have learned quickly how to dodge the sharp hooves. They play with an old rag doll I found amidst my belongings, and I laugh to see their tug-of-war.

After the storms, the sun shines brilliantly and the earth smells fresh and clean.

"It's as if God Himself has washed this beautiful land."

Enrique smiles and crosses himself. Except for that, he now seems as much an *unqua* as Akaiyan, wearing the shells and beads around his neck, donning the ceremonial cape for dances and celebrations. He's even wearing his hair like my beloved husband.

Thomas grows taller and taller. This year he'll turn thirteen, the age of manhood. He's brown as a berry, pulls a bowstring as skilled as any *quottis*, young man, and is learning Croatoan. Mother and I hardly ever see him, except at night to sleep.

My belly rounds ever so slightly. I can feel the life springing up from my womb, though there's no movement yet. Mother sometimes stares at me, raises her eyebrows questioningly but says nothing. I know she's waiting for me to say something but I won't, not yet. Akaiyan is so busy with the *a hots*, with hunting and foraging, that I've not had a moment alone with him, it seems. My "perfect" time to tell him hasn't yet arrived. But I will soon, for before long my child will push its way up from the depths of my womb to make its visible sign upon the world. This morning, we've all been confined inside, for the mightiest of all storms is still raging outside. The thunder booms and the lightning lights up the black sky with an eerie glow. I can hear the *a hots* neighing frantically. Akaiyan has been with them all night, helping Enrique. Even Manteo himself left his solitary lodge and spent the early hours assisting. The roof is half-off the *a hots'* quarters. I can imagine the fear in their gentle souls. I wrap my cape around me and slip outside, almost knocked down by the wind and the rain. I run to the *a hots'* house and push my way inside. But it isn't warm and dry; only rain and wind greet me through the roof, partially torn open by the fury of the storm.

Chapter 20

Stranded On The Shoals

EVERYTHING IS SOAKING WET. The *a hots* pull at their tethers, unnerved by the savagery of nature. The small *squarrena* are huddled in a corner, for the first time showing fear at the chaos around them. Enrique is trying to calm the stallions. Akaiyan re-ties Qui-heiratse, who has broken loose from her halter.

"What can I do?"

The orders follow quickly: help Manteo with Chaunoctay, who kicks at the planked walls: assist with Star and Hoonoch: make sure the *squarrena* don't get trampled. We finally get all of them calmed down and properly tied. Then Enrique and Akaiyan, along with Quayah, who's come to assist, climb the rafters to pull the brush roof back in place and firmly anchor its corners. At long last, the wind and rain no longer invade this sanctuary and, eventually, the storm lessens in intensity. The *a hots* calm down and we feed them extra grain. Teethha, Che-chou and Sooka come out from where they've been hiding and play around our feet. We rub them dry and feed them also.

I'm soaking wet, as are the others. I see Akaiyan staring at me as I hold Sooka and let him lick my face. My face reddens, for I realize my cape has slipped and I'm in my thin sleeping bodice. It clings to my frame and my budding roundness is fully visible. Akaiyan comes to me and takes Sooka out of my arms.

"Little Bird," he whispers, "Why did you not tell me...?"

He places his hand upon my belly. I'm crying then, for this wasn't how I wished to tell him of my precious secret. He moves his hand to cup it under my chin.

"Why are you crying?"

I just shake my head, crying, laughing, clinging to him. I'm sorely embarrassed, for from the rafters Enrique and Quayah are staring, and from Chaunoctay's stall, Manteo watches all.

"Do your parents know?" Akaiyan asks later back at our lodge house. I shake my head.

"I wanted to tell you first."

He gives me a gentle kiss.

"When?"

"Next February."

"I shall pray for a son."

"It might be a daughter. Would that bother you?"

He thinks for a minute.

"*Unqua* prefer sons...," then seeing my face, "but a girl child who is just like you would be most welcome."

Mother takes me in her arms and holds me tightly.

"I knew it, I knew it all along. How are you feeling?"

"Why, I'm perfect, dear Mother. Are you happy for me?"

A flood of tears follow, but I know she's happy. For the

creation of life has always been a cause for celebration, especially now against the painful realization that my father is dying.

He holds my hand, gripping it strongly, which surprises me. I give him hot tea, a ritual we still follow.

"Dear Father, are you gladdened by the news?"

"Indeed... I am... for to have a grandchild delights my heart. Mother knows?"

"Yes. She hugged me and cried."

"Your mother is dealing with a great deal these days."

"Father, if it's a son, I should like to name him after you."

"Arnold is hardly an Indian name, Jess. Have you discussed this with your husband?"

In actuality, I haven't discussed names at all. When I was a child growing up in England, I used to play with Alice and Mary. We'd take our dolls and pretend they were all part of one family. There'd be a father, a mother, and five little children. Each of us had different names for the one boy and five girls; on the gender of the children, at least we agreed. I'd always liked the name William Arnold, including my dear father's name. For girls, I'd preferred Elizabeth Anne, Gwendolyn Jane, Antoinette Mary and Suzanne Emily.

Now, as I carry Akaiyan's child in my womb, those English-sounding names seem somehow inappropriate. My child will have both English and Indian grandparents. I will have to find a name that brings joy and honor to both.

The women of our village gather around me in my newly-discovered state. Wenefrid Powell invites me often to her house to play with her babe. Mistress Steueens, while childless herself, knits and sews delicate infant things for me, humming all the while. Sinopa has laid out *unqua* treasures, clothing made of the softest *ocques*, buckskin, even little booties fashioned like miniature moccasins. The strength I draw from these women is remarkable. We are a clan united, *nickreruroh* and *unqua*, in our joy and expectation. Then comes the bad news. During that last storm, a Spanish ship has foundered upon the treacherous shoals just beyond Croatoan Island. We can see it in the distance, balanced precariously upon those hidden reefs, a gaping hole in its side. It tilts and lists with each wave. Some of our men want to take an *ooshunnawa* and row out, to see what's left and what might be salvaged. Others are dead-set against it. We've placed a patrol along the shoreline near the trees, to wait and see if there are any survivors. We're in a state of alert, for Spanish *conquistadores* are not needed here, in this peaceful paradise we call home.

Chapter 21

The Ghost Ship

FOR THREE DAYS, the Spanish ship rests upon the rocks, impaled on the hidden reef like a gigantic insect pinned by a shaft of stone. The men on post near the shore have seen no one. On the dawn of the fourth day, several *unqua* and English decide to row out. They bring weapons, just in case, and tow an empty *ooshunnawa* to bring back whatever is salvageable.

Akaiyan and Enrique are among those chosen to go. Akaiyan kisses me a fond goodbye and I wave as the canoes pull away from the beach. All that day I fret and pace the sandy dunes, staring at the wreck and wondering what they'll find. By late afternoon, the *ooshunnawa* row back to us, the third one laden down with goods. I run to greet them all, watching the men drag the canoes up on the shore and unload the goods.

There are boxes full of preserved food, many tools and ropes which we can use, some charts and maps, even some silver and gold coins. Several of our men are carrying Spanish

firearms. A grand find is a cache of dried powder for the weapons and boxes of ammunition. We help load the two travois behind Qui-heiratse and Chaunoctay, and bring the treasures back to the village.

Later that evening, we gather around the fire and listen to the men tell of their adventure. Enrique is the story teller and I, the translator for all our friends.

"It was a dangerous crossing, taking all our strength to keep on course. We tied the *ooshunnawa* to the sides and climbed on board. There was no one alive - a big mystery. We discovered several dead bodies below deck; one was obviously *el capitán*. He'd been shot through the heart. There were definite signs of a struggle. Below deck were several empty compartments where *los caballos* had been quartered. But there were no *caballos* at all. The entire ship was like a ghost vessel, haunted by spirits. We were glad to leave."

The *unqua* women hide their faces in their hands when I translate about the spirits. *Unqua*, I've learned, are very superstitious. Souls of the dead may wander and cause mischief if the proper prayers and rituals haven't been carried out. Prayers are necessary to help them on their journey toward the Great Spirit. Without them, souls are like the undead, plaguing those still alive, playing all sorts of tricks and causing much havoc.

I'm concerned not only about the missing *soldados*, but about the *a hots*. What happened to them? Were they washed overboard and drowned in the big storm? Did any of them manage to swim to shore? If so, why haven't they been sighted?

Master Steueens and Master Clement think the Spanish galleon was set upon by English or else, by pirates, those bloodthirsty brigands who owe allegiance to no country, seeking only to plunder and loot. Perhaps a battle was fought upon the high seas, the galleon boarded, the men taken prisoner. Perhaps the huge storm came upon them suddenly, and all were lost. Or maybe the few remaining *soldados* turned on their *capitán*, thinking to steal whatever bounty was left. No one was watching their drift toward the shoals, and they were suddenly dashed upon the rocks. Were the men, like the *a hots*, swept overboard? Did one kind *soldado*, like my dear Enrique, free the horses and lead them to the upper deck, giving them a chance to swim to safety? So many questions and no answers!

I suppose the mystery will never be revealed. Our brave men propose to row out again and sink the ship, tearing more huge holes in its sides to let the sea water rush in. They fear to leave it impaled there as a beacon for pirate ships, luring them in to explore further. Even Father, sick as he is, applauds the idea of sinking it. So out they row again and before two more days pass, the wreck is engulfed by the sea and settles to its watery grave.

But an uneasiness pervades our quiet village. Could Spanish invaders be lurking somewhere in the woodlands further up the coast? Might they, even now, be finding their way down toward Croatoan Island? Manteo calls for more guards, set up at intervals to keep a watchful eye. The children are forbidden to play outside the boundaries of the village. The hunting parties range only so far. And Enrique doesn't ride Diablo up and down the dunes with reckless abandon the way he used to do.

We're a village on alert, listening for strange sounds in the night, going about our business warily. The *unqua* carry their bows at all times; the *nickreruroh* men wear their firearms tucked in their belts. It's a time of fear and trepidation for us all.

The spoils from the wreck are divided up among all the families, Indian and English alike. Mother exclaims over her share of the preserved meats and spices.

"How wonderful!" she cries, holding up ginger, pepper, salt and dried sage. "Now my cooking will be tasty again."

Father coughs from his bed, trying to talk and laugh at the same time.

"Your cooking was always delicious... my dear Joyce...."

"You flatter me, Arnold, for I know how bland it's been."

The fact that he eats very little is not forgotten in the lines of worry around her mouth. She sprinkles a little pepper in her palm and bends down to let him taste it. But the pungent smell sets him to coughing again, the bloody froth with which he stains the rag scaring us all.

Chapter 22

Why The 'Possum Plays Dead

"I WILL TELL YOU TWO STORIES," says Sinopa.

I sit across from her in her lodge house where she's invited me. It's a great honor for me to be here, and I'm tingling with excitement. Mother sends me away after Father has such a fit of coughing that we all panic. When at last he falls asleep, she gives me a kiss and pushes me out the door.

"This is no place for you today," she says, her shoulders bent with weariness. "Go and find something happy to do."

I would go to the *a hots*, my place of sanctuary, there to play with *los lobitos* or the foals, but Sinopa beckons.

"Your father grows... worse," she says in broken English, for Manteo has been teaching her. I nod my head.

"Come," she turns and walks to her lodge house.

She brews me some tea, rather strong and made of herbal leaves. She sits across from me smoking her long *oosquaana*, then fans the smoke in my direction. When I start to cough, she leans forward.

"Is not the... smoke... good for you?"

I shake my head. But she keeps on smoking, her only concession to blow the clouds away from me. Then she begins talking in Croatoan.

"Your father will die. It is written in the stars. But do not be distressed. For all things must pass from this life to the next. He will not be lonely."

She surprises me by suddenly leaning forward and patting my stomach. She smiles.

"Good, good, an *utserosta* will join our people together. Good, good. Now I will talk and you listen. One day a wolf came into the *unqua's* village and stole their corn meal. He left his tracks for them to find. So they hid and when he came again, they beat him with big sticks until he ran howling, back to his home in the north. The corn meal fell from his mouth as he ran, leaving a white trail like stars in *oosottoo*. Yes... yes?"

"We call those stars the Milky Way."

"We call them *Geh-oonut-santunyi*."

She rocks where she sits, laughing softly.

"You like my story?"

"Oh, yes."

"I will tell you another. One day, the rabbit and the *che-ra*, opossum, were looking for a wife, each to wed because they were lonely. The rabbit ran first to a town where there were many animals. He said he had an order that each one was to marry right away. They all took *kateocca* and the rabbit got his mate. By the time the *che-ra* got there, there was no one left for him to marry. The other animals thought he would steal their mates, so they beat him with sticks. He fell over and lay very still, so he could get away afterwards. That's why the *che-ra* plays dead whenever an enemy is near."

She chuckles some more and offers me a puff on her pipe. When I shake my head, she smiles.

"*Nickreruroh* think *oo-teighne* is bad?"

"No, the men like to smoke. But it's bad for babes."

"Aahh."

Then she stares at me and her face gets serious.

"You are glad for this child?"

"Very glad."

"Good, good. Akaiyan is glad. Manteo is glad. I am very happy."

Then she gets up and pushes me out her door.

"I will tell your son lots of stories. Now, go, go, get names, good *unqua* names that *nickreruroh* will also like. Think hard."

My heart is lightened when I leave her house. What she says about my father is right. Manteo has told me many times that death comes to all, and the Great Spirit watches over us. There's nothing to fear. How I wish my dear mother could find her strength in the *unqua* beliefs.

I find Akaiyan with the *a hots*, grooming Diablo while the wolf cubs play around his feet.

"I was with Sinopa," I tell him. "She made me tea and told me stories."

He smiles.

"We have all heard Sinopa's stories. What else did she say?"

"That Father will die."

"Oh, Little Bird, are you sad?"

I feel the tears spring to my eyes.

"Yes, but not the way you think. I know he's going to die, but I believe his spirit will live on. I'm very sad he won't know my child, our child...."

Akaiyan puts down the stalk brush and takes me in his arms. I lean against his chest, listening to his heartbeat, feeling his warmth.

"When I'm with you, I'm not afraid."

"We must think of names for our child," he says, kissing me gently. "I will let you make that choice."

"I have two," I tell him then. He takes my hands in his.

"And what are they?"

"Caun-reha, if it's a boy. It means panther and that's the closest to lyon I can get."

He nods his head.

"And if a girl?"

"Oohahn-ne, soft like the down of a goose."

Akaiyan laughs suddenly, "and what of English names?"

"William Arnold and Suzanne Emily."

Then we both laugh.

Chapter 23

Un Soldado y Un Caballo

THREE DAYS LATER, the *unqua* bring in a solitary Spanish soldier, his uniform in rags hanging from his body. He's covered with bruises and sores.

He must think they're going to kill him, for he falls to his knees sobbing with relief when he sees the English gather around.

"*Inglés, inglés*," he cries, for we're less fearsome to him that the Indians. Enrique pulls him to his feet, but he doesn't recognize him as a *compadre*, for my friend is *unqua* in every way.

"*No me mates*." he says, wiping a hand across his face. If he were a grown man, I wouldn't feel sorry for him, never forgetting how the Spanish treated Akaiyan and me at the garrison. But he's a young boy about twelve, with pale blue eyes and dirty blond hair. Of course, we won't kill him. Mother hesitates for but an instant, then goes over to him, placing her arm about his shoulders.

"What's your name?" she says gently.

He looks about wildly, deciding maybe to make a dash for it. But where would he go, in the middle of an island, in a hostile land? His legs tremble and he looks about to collapse.

"*¿Cuál es tu nombre?*" I ask, stepping forward.

He stares at me. Am I English or Indian? How can I speak in Spanish?

"*Mi nombre es Jess,*" I continue, then sweep my hand around at the others. "We are *inglés e indios*, living together in peace."

"*Yo soy Carlos de Avilar,*" he stammers. "*¿Hablas tú español?*"

"*Sí, y mi amigo, Enrique también.*"

Enrique comes forward and extends his hand. The young boy takes it hesitantly. They talk together rapidly for a few moments, neither our good folk or the *unqua* understanding a word.

"It seems," says Enrique turning to face us, "that Carlos was on that ship, steward to *el capitán*. He's the one who freed *los caballos*. He untied them during the height of the storm and led them topside. When the ship rammed against the rocks, he forced them overboard to swim to safety. Then he, too, jumped."

"So he doesn't know what happened to his *capitán?*"

"No. There was much fighting. Pirates had boarded and killed most of the crew. He had hidden below with *los caballos*. There was an argument between *el capitán* and some pirates. That's all he knows before the ship ran aground."

"*¿Qué les pasó a los caballos?*"

The boy shakes his head when Enrique questions him.

"There's only one *caballo* left. Of all six, he knows of only one which survived."

"Where is it?"

"Back in the woods. It's still loose, but he's been feeding it."

"We have to rescue it," I turn to Akaiyan. "We can't leave it to die."

Akaiyan and Enrique, together with Quayah and his friend, Guytui, quickly mount up and gallop off into the woods. Mother leads the young boy to our lodge house. There, she gives him some food which he gobbles up. Father stares at him from his bed, coughing constantly, then lying back down again.

"What... have you brought us... Joyce. A lost soul...?"

"A young boy, Arnold, not an enemy soldier, just a young boy like our Thomas."

"Aahh...." Father takes a sip of water from the cup she holds.

"And... what do we... do with him?"

The boy stares all around, for the English, his enemy, are decidedly not the monsters he's heard about all his life. For the first time in a long while, he relaxes, the tension draining from his body.

"*Inglés*," he says then, "*¿viven ustedes entre los indios?*"

"*Sí, es nuestra gente ahora.*"

"*¿Por qué?*"

"*Porque son nuestros amigos. Porque lo queremos.*"

But he shakes his head.

"*Los indios... salvajes, ellos matan a nuestros soldados.*"

"*No estos indios.* They are *unqua*, we are like *unqua*."

It's all too much for the boy. He puts his face in his hands and I can see his shoulders heave with sobs.

"He must rest, Jess," Mother whispers. "Tell him I've made him a place where he can sleep."

When I tell him, he nods, then goes to lie down where Mother points. Almost before he lays his head down, his eyes close and he's asleep. Mother gives a huge sigh. She walks over and takes my hands in hers.

"We're a family of many different souls," she says, "English, Indian and Spanish. Who would have thought it...."

"I think Our Lord meant for this to be, Mother."

"Do you?"

"Yes," I reply, giving her a gentle kiss on the cheek. "For men shouldn't fight each other, but live in peace and harmony."

"If only it were true," she whispers, covering the sleeping youth, "if only it were true."

Chapter 24

Utchar

WHAT A SORRY-LOOKING HORSE they bring in. His ribs stick out from his sides, almost like barrel-staves. His hide is dull like old leather, and his head hangs down. He doesn't seem to have the energy to gallop, but trots listlessly after Qui-heiratse.

Carlos is awake and goes out to see. When they rein up in front of Mother's lodge, he runs up and throws his arms about the *a hots*. The animal neighs softly and a spark of fire seems to charge through him. He pushes his head against the boy, nuzzling him. Carlos looks around.

"*¿Tienes tú una manzana?*" he asks and Mother goes back inside, returning with the small apple. Carlos holds out his hand and the *a hots* takes it gratefully.

"Why does he look like that?" I ask Carlos in Spanish. "He's so thin. Is he sick?"

"They beat him. He is... a gelding. They think him worthless."

So, in truth, *un caballo* who can't make babes isn't worthy of proper care? The Spanish are a cruel lot.

"But how did he survive the raging sea?"

Carlos shakes his head.

"I do not know," he replies. "His will to live is very strong."

He strokes the *a hots* gently, with much love.

"*Era mi favorito.* When he escaped over the side, I followed. I grabbed his rope and he pulled me."

I look in amazement at this wretched animal, mistreated and loved only by a young boy. I think of Diablo and Thunderer. What will they do to him?

"Stallions do not fight geldings," Enrique whispers in my ear, as if reading my very thoughts. "They're not competition for the mares."

Enrique and Carlos lead the horse to the animal lodge. They tether him far away from the two stallions anyway, then give him plenty of food and fresh water. Qui-heiratse, tethered nearby, stretches her neck to sniff at him. The gelding sniffs back, then turns his attention to eating.

"What's his name?"

Carlos shrugs.

"I never gave him one."

"We must give him a name and make him feel at home."

The boy stares at me.

"You are not Spanish, yet you speak our tongue. You are *inglés*, yet you dress like *los indios*. I am confused."

"*Mi nombre es Jess,*" I say again. "I am married to Akaiyan."

The boy shakes his head and turns back to the horse. He begins rubbing his hands over its back.

"They beat him and gave him little food. I had to steal

to feed him enough."

"Why did they take him along if they didn't like him?"

"He was a trade, to pay passage for one of the crew. The others laughed when they saw him brought on board. But I... I saw *su espíritu. Tiene fuego y viveza dentro de él,* he has a hidden fire in him."

"That's it," I cry. "We'll call him Utchar, the *unqua* word for fire."

"Utchar," Carlos whispers. "I like that."

We leave Carlos curled up in the stall next to Utchar. The animal is still eating. Akaiyan clicks his teeth as we walk away.

"This *a hots* is not fit to ride."

"We have to fatten him up."

He shakes his head.

"How did he survive such a long swim. Only the strong could make such a swim. And where are the others? If they died, why did he not die?"

I can't answer him, for I don't know. Perhaps, as Carlos says, the others didn't have the fire in their bellies the way Utchar did. Perhaps hunger and abuse make the spirit strong, even in an *a hots*. My heart goes out to the sad little gelding. First he is made less than a male, then he's laughed at and starved. Only Carlos loved him and he paid him back. He saved Carlos' life by pulling him to shore. There's no greater love than that, to save the life of a friend.

Utchar settles in and feels right at home. By the end of the second day, he's eaten his portion of food and Qui-hei-ratse's too, stretching his long neck over to reach her tray. He greets Carlos with great affection, thrusting his head against the boy's chest, waiting to be scratched behind the ears. He plays with Star and Hoonoch. It's easy to see he's contented.

For the most part, Diablo and Thunderer pay him little heed, laying back their ears only when he comes too close as he's led past them. For he's the most inquisitive *a hots* I've ever seen, poking his nose into everything. He makes me laugh.

"He's like a child who sees the flames and wants to touch them, even though he's been warned not to. And then one day, he does."

"What happens?" Akaiyan asks.

"He gets a burned nose," I laugh, "and runs back to his mother."

Chapter 25

The Dream

THE *UNQUA* ARE BECOMING a tribe of horse people. Every day, at least four or five of them slip into the animal compound to marvel at the *a hots*. Mothers take their young children; men and women manage to walk by the area where they're kept, putting aside their duties for a few moments, a bundle of kindling wood placed to one side, a line of fish draped carefully over the fence post, to pat the sleek animals. They're all growing fat from the treats being fed them, including Utchar. His sides are beginning to fill out, his coat gleams.

The young women, especially, come to admire Thunderer and Diablo, staring at them, enthralled by their size and masculine parts. I think they'd be embarrassed but no, they point and giggle just like schoolgirls, just like Mary, Alice and I used to do back in England when we talked about possible suitors. Whenever they see Enrique or Carlos, they giggle even more and run away red-faced, their hands covering their faces. Enrique laughs but there's one, in particular, who has caught his eye. She's named Te-lah-tai, with jet-black hair and deep brown eyes. She's about fifteen, quite comely, and I believe Enrique is enchanted.

"Soon he will ask her to be his *kateocca*," Akaiyan smiles.

"Do you think so?"

He nods his head.

"Te-lah-tai will bear him many fine sons."

I blush. For my own sweet babe has awakened in his world of darkness and moves insistently in my womb, announcing his forthcoming presence. He kicks and thrusts his legs, flails with his arms and rises up from my belly, often interrupting my sleep. Oh, why don't babes sleep when their parents do, instead of keeping them up half the night?

Akaiyan and Enrique have been teaching the young boys and men how to ride and now, even the girls are clamoring for lessons. He leads Qui-heiratse and Utchar, the two calmest, and lets them mount up sitting astride the broad backs, feeling the delicious newness of being so high. Then slowly he leads them around the village, first in a walk, then a trot. They're enthralled. When they become more experienced, he and Carlos teach them how to groom and clean out the stalls. *Unqua*, I've found, are enthusiastic learners.

Last night, I dreamed about Eleanor. It was a strange dream. In it, she was walking in a field of flowers, little Virginia running before her. Behind Eleanor walked a strange and shadowy figure. I thought it was Ananyas and heard her call out his name. Several times she called, but the figure remained shrouded in mist. She stopped at one point and began painting her name on the rough bark of trees. I don't know where the paint came from, but she dipped her fingers again and again in bright colors of red, blue and yellow.

"Eleanor Dare," she wrote over and over, "Eleanor Dare."

Then the scene shifted and the meadow grew brighter. Horses appeared and galloped with thunderous hooves across the field. They rode up into the sky, trailing streams of fire. Ananyas was riding one of them. Eleanor raised her hands to the sky and suddenly, the *a hots* disappeared, the sky grew black and rain began to fall. I awoke crying and drenched in sweat. Akaiyan stirred and mumbled something in his sleep. I felt my child move in my womb, stretching his little legs. Through the darkness I heard the soft neigh of an *a hots*, the short sharp yip of one of the wolf cubs, then silence again.

This morning I think, where are you now, sweet Eleanor? Have you arrived safely at your destination? Is George Howe there to greet you, so manly and self-assured? Are you, even now, carving a new home out of the wilderness, making a safe haven among the brilliance of this untamed land? What's happened since we left you last April? It's now early November, in the year of Our Lord, 1589. My child grows in my womb; the month of my birthing approaches rapidly, only three months from now; the air grows colder and the wind whips snowflakes across our island from sound to sea, from sea to sound.

Enrique confides in me a week later that he might wish to ask for Te-lah-tai's hand in marriage. It's a strange thing, after all, to think in such civilized ways, for the *unqua* don't have such elaborate ceremonies.

"What should I do?"

"Her father is dead, so I suppose you must ask her mother."

Te-lah-tai's mother is a formidable woman, short and heavy-set, with eyes like steel. She has always scared me just a little, so I can imagine how poor Enrique must feel.

"Are you sure?" I ask him one afternoon.

He sighs.

"I will never get home to my beloved *España*. I must make a life for myself here. I am, after all, becoming an *unqua* like you."

I laugh.

"I don't envy you."

Enrique washes himself carefully in the stream and puts on the buckskin that Akaiyan has given him. He pulls his hair back and places a new feather.

"How do I look?" he asks.

"So handsome," I sigh, clasping my hands together in fun. "She will surely give you her daughter to wed."

He squares his shoulders, then marches over to Te-lah-tai's lodge house. There are no loud screams, no angry banging of pots and kettles. Only *silencio*. When at last he returns, he looks both happy and worried.

"What's the matter?" I ask. "Did she turn you away?"

"*Al contrario*," he replies with a frown. "She looked like she wanted to wed me herself. But she's agreed to give me Te-lah-tai. She just wants Chaunoctay as a dowry present."

I gasp.

"What are you going to do?"

He shrugs his shoulders and quickly crosses himself. "I think *un caballo* is a fair price for a beautiful maiden, don't you? *Espero no tener problemas con la suegra*."

Chapter 26

Wolf Training

WOLF TRAINING HAS BEGUN. Enrique has undertaken his task with great seriousness. Thoughts of marriage are put aside as he deals with the three rapidly growing pups. Already, they look like young adults, long-legged, with silver-tinged fur. But they're much fatter than their poor mother ever was. They wag their tails like dogs, also. However, they've several bad habits, like chasing the animals and nipping our heels when we walk past. Last week, Teethha pinned a chicken to the ground and was worrying it with his sharp white teeth. We rescued the poor frightened hen, but Manteo threatened to shoot Teethha with his bow if we didn't start some discipline. I know he's worried that we can ever turn wild wolves into tame and loyal companions.

Each morning, bright and early, I can hear Enrique and Carlos with the cubs. They've put them on leashes instead of letting them run free. The cubs whine and strain at the collars, but they can't get loose. Then Enrique takes each one and gives him a lesson in manners. First he must sit, then stay, then walk at heel. If anyone nips, he gets a sharp smack. Enrique walks them past the chickens, who flutter and squawk in terror. Sooka and Che-Chou do quite nicely, but Teethha lunges and almost pulls Enrique's arm off. Teethha is punished, sitting in disgrace all by himself while the others are rewarded with a treat. He raises his small muzzle and howls his misery. Moan after moan assails our ears until we all feel sorry for him. The next day, the lessons begin over again.

Enrique's audience grows as news of the training spreads through the village. It's almost impossible to expect the little wolf cubs to pay attention, when so many distractions are around them. The *unqua* are fascinated with *los lobitos*, as much so as with the *a hots*. No one has ever seen a live wolf up close before. No one has ever thought of training one. Though admired from afar for their prowess and skill, wolves are a dangerous enemy to this peaceful way of life. They steal the little animals, and have even stalked hunters when the winter snows are deep and the game has vanished.

But little by little, the cubs learn good manners. Teethha, the largest, proves the most difficult. He receives many smacks and loses out on many treats until he learns how to behave.

True to his word, Enrique invites Te-lah-tai's mother to the animal compound, there to present her with Chaunoctay, his wedding gift. Manteo and Sinopa are present. The *unqua* clap their hands and stamp their feet in approval. Akaiyan didn't formally give a dowry to my parents when we wed, for Mother and Father declined, saying this village home was present enough. I know this has bothered him for some time, so on that same day, he leads Sooka to my mother and hands her the leash. She looks startled.

"It's his dowry for me, Mother," I explain.

She frowns.

"What shall I...?"

"Smile and take him," I continue. "For the wolf cubs are considered quite a prize."

She takes the leash from Akaiyan, thanks him and ties Sooka to a post outside. Then Akaiyan goes away, to come back in a few moments with several necklaces of copper and shells strung together. He hands them to Mother.

"Why, thank you," she says. He waits, so she places them around her neck. Akaiyan smiles.

"You've made him very happy, Mother."

"I'm happy as long as you are," she says softly, then turns and goes inside to tend to Father.

Te-lah-tai's mother agrees to keep Chaunoctay with the rest of the *a hots*. She proudly brings the other women to see the mare, explaining eagerly how this one is hers. They swarm around Chaunoctay, who at first is skittish and fretful. But the *unqua* pet her gently and feed her choice cornmeal and oats, so she allows them to stroke her soft muzzle and pat her fat sides. The women admire little Star and Hoonoch, nodding their heads in satisfaction at the growing number of *a hots*. Chaunoctay is swelling in her pregnancy by Thunderer. Te-lah-tai's mother has made a good bargain with Enrique, for the foal will be hers as well.

Wolf lessons continue and life goes on. The days are short, darkness descends quickly and soon we see more white flakes of snow. Winter has come swiftly to our fair island, much swifter than when I was a child in England. Snow covers the ground, the wind whips in fury off the dark sea and we wrap our bearskin capes tightly around us. All Autumn, the *unqua* gathered wood, the children piling the kindling into huge mounds next to each lodge house. This fuel is essential to the fires which will warm us through the long, cold months. There is an urgency to see that everything is in order before ice covers all. Fingers freeze and noses burn from the cold. We nod as we pass each other, barely engaging in conversation in our haste to complete each task. By early December, Thomas has turned fourteen and, just before our own Christmastide, I reach my seventeenth birthday.

Chapter 27

An Unfortunate Incident

MOTHER HAS FINALLY allowed Sooka inside. It's much too cold for him to be tied up while the winds blow and the snow falls. She's made a little corner for him with a mat where he can lie. In truth, he provides company for Father whenever she has to go outside, trotting over the moment she leaves to jump upon the end of Father's bed. Sooka is much smaller than either Teethha or Che-Chou, and has the nicest disposition of the three. I rarely think of him anymore as a *squarrena*, but like one of our friendly dogs back in England. I know Father's comforted by his presence, and I often catch him petting Sooka, who licks his hand.

December passes into a cold and bitter January. Sometimes the wind howls so strongly that our entrance covering flaps loudly and seems almost to tear off. In both our lodge and Mother's, Akaiyan has fastened a large bear skin over the entrance as added protection.

The *a hots* are warm enough, for Enrique and Carlos have

secured the animal shelter, reinforcing the roof and sealing the cracks. It always smells warm and comforting inside; the richness of the *a hots* and the sweet scent of grain linger like a perfume to me. Teethha and Che-Chou play outside a lot, for they love to romp in the snow. Teethha is still disobedient, chasing the children and nipping at their heels.

Then one day we find a dead chicken, its feathers bloodied and torn. There's a trail of red pawprints and Manteo tracks then back to the wolf cubs, to Teethha.

"We can not have this," he says, his voice grim and stern. "An animal that kills is not welcome in our village."

Against my protests, he takes Teethha on a leash and disappears into the woods. A pain strikes my heart like the blow of a hammer, for when he returns Teethha isn't with him and he still has his bow.

"What have you done with him?" I ask.

Akaiyan pulls on my hand. "It is not your place to question," he whispers.

Manteo stares at me.

"Little Bird, he is dead. I shot him with my arrow. He cannot be allowed to kill."

An anger springs suddenly inside me. How dare he kill my wolf cub? It was I who rescued him, who first heard them all whimpering from hunger. The female wolf's spirit asked me to protect them, and I made a promise.

"I would have trained him," I say with vehemence. "You didn't have to kill him!"

I'm so angry at Teethha's death, I'm not even thinking. I've never questioned the *unqua* way of life before this moment. In my unhappiness, I can't see the logic of Manteo's thinking. I stamp my foot like a petulant child, then turn and walk back to my lodge house. I turn my back when Akaiyan

comes in, refusing to talk even to him. Tears run down my cheeks at the thought of little Teethha. What's one chicken, after all? There are many. He would have learned; I could have taught him.

There's silence behind me, a silence so heavy that I can't ignore it. I turn my head, thinking to see Akaiyan. But it's Manteo himself, sitting cross-legged on the bearskin rug which covers the floor of our house.

"Oh," I gasp, wishing I haven't been crying. I don't want the great chief to see me this way.

"You loved him."

It isn't a question, but a statement. Slowly I nod my head.

"Sometimes the things we love most are taken from us. It is no one's fault."

How strange. I remember those words from long ago... from Eleanor before she left us: 'when we least expect, life takes from us those we love.' I cover my face with my hands.

"The *unqua* are a peaceful people. We are the earth's caretakers, seeking to do no harm to any living creature. We hunt only for food and, when necessary, to protect ourselves and those we love. The wolf cub was not learning. He killed once, he would kill again. The others would smell the blood on him and their instincts would take over. The next time might be a child...," he pauses, "... your child, perhaps."

His words penetrate my grief. I slowly nod my head, my eyes still wet with tears. Manteo gets up and stands silently before me. I hold my head up high staring into his eyes, like silver points of light.

"Little Bird," he says softly. "You are not yet *unqua*. You have much still to learn."

Then he turns and leaves me alone with my thoughts.

Chapter 28

Carlos Is Captured

I MOURN THE LOSS of little Teethha, for I truly loved him. Che-Chou senses his loss more than Sooka, who lives now in my parents' lodge. Che-Chou searches the animal compound, sniffing here, sniffing there, raising his muzzle to howl his sadness. But like all animals, he soon forgets and follows Enrique and Carlos around once more, fetching sticks that they throw, tugging on the rag doll.

I have reconciled myself to the wisdom of Manteo's words. An animal which has tasted blood will surely kill again. I hug my hands around my belly, shuddering at the thought that one day Teethha might have crept upon my babe's cradle, seizing him. Better the loss of a single wolf cub than a human child. I turn my thoughts away from sadness and look toward the future; my hour of birthing draws ever close. Then one morning when there's no snow falling, we hear loud cries and great alarm. We all rush outside to see Carlos being held in the vise-like grip of a large Spaniard. Where did he come from? How did he survive our coldest days alone in the woods? Carlos struggles in vain, but the large *soldado* pulls him backwards toward the cover of the trees. Carlos is screaming,

"*¡Apúrate, apúrate!*"

El enemigo points a firearm at Enrique, waving it furiously in the air and cursing loudly. Enrique is helpless to do anything. The man is huge and Carlos small. It seems a lost cause.

We watch in horror as the *soldado* drags our newest friend away. In anguish, we see him disappear into the thickness of the trees which, even without leaves, grow close enough together to provide cover. Enrique comes running over to us.

"He came from the woods. Carlos was taken before he had a chance. I think he's from the shipwreck. Who knows how many others are out there. We must do something!"

"Why didn't he steal a *caballo* instead of Carlos?"

Enrique gestures helplessly.

"Perhaps he didn't have time. Carlos must have startled him, so he grabbed him instead."

"What can we do?"

Manteo strides over, his bear cape wrapped tightly around him.

"We will go after them," he says decisively. Then, pointing at me, "you go inside. For your time is close."

In earlier days, I might have been embarrassed, but not now. I nod my head, give Akaiyan a quick kiss on the cheek and watch them mount the *a hots*. Enrique, Akaiyan, Manteo and Towaye ride out of our village, hot in pursuit. If he's only one *hombre*, he doesn't stand a chance.

The men and women gather in small groups.

"We must stand guard," cautions Roger Bayley, "in case it's a trick to lure the Indians out. Gather your firearms and post a watch."

Our whole village is on alert again. The women gather the children and bring them inside. Mother returns to Father's bedside. I decide to remain with the *a hots* and Che-Chou.

Inside with the animals, I feel the peace I seek so desperately. Star greets me by pushing her head against my fat stomach. Hoonoch nips at her rump. Chaunoctay eats, content in the fullness of her own pregnancy. Utchar whinnies a greeting. I play with the foals and absent-mindedly pet Che-Chou. Suddenly, he growls and the hairs on the back of his neck stand up. Startled, I whisper,

"What is it, Che-Chou?"

He keeps a low growling, standing stiff-legged and staring at the door. My heart begins racing in my chest. I pick up a small hoe and move as quickly as I can to the side, where I can't be easily seen. The door flap is pushed to one side and a figure, wrapped against the cold, comes cautiously inside. I gasp.

For it's another *soldado*, not as large as the first. I bite my lip til the blood runs. So it was a trick, after all, to lure the *unqua* away. While they're off chasing the one who took Carlos, this other sneaks in to steal our beloved horses. I grip the hoe until my knuckles are white. Is he alone? Are there others behind him? How did he get past the English? How can I fight him, a woman awkward and large with child?

Che-Chou is growling most ferociously now. Little silver-coat, I think, scare him away please. The enemy is wrapped in old blankets, ragged and torn. He freezes at the sight of Che-Chou, then takes a heavy stick from behind his back. He won't use a firearm, I think, for that will bring the village down upon him. He plans to beat little Che-Chou over the head. Surely he can hear my heart pounding in my breast? As he passes me, I raise my arms to swing the hoe down upon him. He turns to face me. Suddenly there's a muted "thump," and the *soldado* gasps, then crumples slowly to the ground. Protruding from his back is an arrow and framed in the entrance stands Quayah, the bow in his hand, his eyes large with terror.

Chapter 29

The Celebration

I DON'T EVEN SCREAM. Perhaps there are others still lurking outside. I pull Quayah inside quickly and we hug each other. He's only about a year younger than Thomas. He quickly slips another arrow into the bowstring, motions me to the back of the lodge and crouches low, watching the entrance. We wait for what seems like an eternity. But no one else enters. At long last, Quayah lifts the door flap and peers outside. There's nothing but snow beginning to fall again.

At that point we hear the *a hots* returning. Loud whoops and cries precede their coming. From out of the trees gallop the horses. There are double riders on one. Carlos is clutching Enrique's waist. Towaye is whooping loudly in victory. I grab Quayah's arm and we go outside to greet them.

The entire village comes out to hear the news. First, Manteo tells us how they tracked the enemy, having to dismount at certain points for the trees were so thick. They came upon him in a short time. Carlos was rigid with fear. The *soldado* waved his weapon and threatened to shoot Carlos. Enrique tried talking to him but it did no good. Finally Towaye drew an arrow from his bow, hitting the man in the leg. He dropped his weapon, Carlos fell to the ground and a second arrow pierced the rogue's throat.

"It is done," Manteo says, dismounting and clapping Carlos on the back. It's rare to see him show such affection. Towaye grunts and dismisses his prowess, though the *unqua* gather around and murmur their praise. No one knows of the body lying inside the *a hots'* shelter house. I quickly pull Akaiyan to one side and tell him. He stares long and hard at his younger brother, then grabs his arm, pulling him over to Manteo. At first, no one can can't believe how they were tricked. Anger burns in their faces, then relief and finally, great joy. Quayah is hoisted high upon Towaye's shoulders and a celebration is called for.

"There were only two," Akaiyan tells me, "*katichlei*, rogues. They survived the Spanish wreck, swimming to shore further up the coast. They made their way down toward our village, seeing their chance to steal from us."

Quayah is a hero. Even though it's cold and snow is falling, a big fire is lit in the center of the village and we all gather around. A large circle is formed with Quayah in the center. Arms are linked and even the children are included. The *unqua* stamp their feet and sing, chanting words of victory. Towaye and some others shake large gourds and rattles; even the women beat on their pots and kettles with sticks.

Quayah stands in the center trying to remain solemn and serious. The boys run up and touch him, as if taking his strength upon themselves. At one point, one of the *quottis* throws off his bearskin covering and dances, naked except for a loincloth. He flings snow upon his body, seemingly unaffected by the cold. I can almost feel the energy flowing from the outer circle toward the center. Manteo steps into the center at one point, crouching first to the ground, then standing and flinging his arms heavenward. He does this twice to signal two victories over the enemy. Quayah is lifted to his shoulders, then Manteo dances around holding his son there. Everybody cheers. There's so much noise that we can hear the *a hots* neighing in alarm, so Enrique and Carlos slip back to feed and calm them down. Che-Chou runs around barking and so does Sooka. We all laugh in great delight at the cubs.

The celebration lasts all day. The *unqua* drink a fermented beer with makes many of them drunk. Even our *nickreruroh* are staggering slightly from the potent brew. The body of the *soldado* is speedily removed. I see a group of men heading toward the woods, to bury it and that of the first man. They will lie in unmarked graves, with no one to mourn them.

All this excitement is too much for Mother, who has slept fitfully since Father first became sick. She retires to their lodge to rest herself and comfort him. I go to help Mistress Steueens brew them honey tea and make a stew. As I leave the celebration, I feel Akaiyan's hand slip into mine. He pulls me close and brushes his lips upon my cheek.

"My brother will be a fine *entequos*, man, some day."

"You should be very proud of him."

He looks at me.

"What is that?"

"To have good feelings, to admire him."

He nods his head.

"We all feel that way... about him. Oh, Little Bird, what would have happened if he had not shot his arrow?"

I give a shudder.

121

"I don't know," I answer, feeling a strange aching in my back. "Oh," I gasp, as the ache becomes a pain which seizes me.

"What is it?"

"I don't know." I stand there for a moment. "I think... I think, maybe... our babe is coming."

Akaiyan walks me slowly to our lodge house. I sink gratefully upon the bed.

"Do not move," he says, looking worried, "I will fetch help."

But I have no thoughts of moving, for the pains have become steady and wrack my frame again and again. Thoughts of Eleanor, of Margaret Harvye in their birthings flash through my mind. But then I can think no more, for the god of fire tears at me and I am at once his victim, his lover, his mate, and he consumes me.

Chapter 30

A Daughter Is Born

NOTHING I EVER WATCHED of a birth prepares me for my own. As I lie there wracked in pain, it seems to me that death is a blessing and life is the anguish or rather, the bringing forth of life.

Mother is by my side, wiping my face with a cool cloth, and I detect Mistress Steueens's warm presence like a clucking hen.

"Where's Akaiyan?" I whisper at one point and Mother tells me he's outside, pacing back and forth like all expectant fathers are supposed to do.

"And Father?"

"He waits in our lodge for good news to come."

I lie back upon the pillow. Mother has loosened my clothing and made me as comfortable as she can.

But there's no comfort. I try not to cry out against the ravages of pain but at the end, I can't help myself. The babe is turned the wrong way, Mother says worriedly, conferring in whispers with Mistress Steueens.

"Let me see," says that goodwife and she kneels by my side.

"Now, little Jess, I will have to lay hands upon your belly and try to turn your child within your womb. Are you a brave girl?"

In my haze of pain I can see two figures kneeling by my bedside, one Mistress Steueens, the other, Sinopa. She is praying to the gods to help speed the birth of my son, my child. Mistress Steueens's hands are huge. Gentle though she tries to be, when she moves my babe inside me, I am torn asunder. My lips are bitten and bleeding but she eventually succeeds. The child grudgingly shifts position, the passage opens to the world and, after several long and agonizing hours, my child is finally born. I lie back exhausted while Mother cleans the babe.

"Let me see my son," I call out weakly.

"I'm afraid I can't do that," smiles Mother, "for you have a daughter. God has blessed you with a beautiful little girl."

"Oh," is all I can manage to say, taking the tiny babe from her. How fragile, how small, to cause such terrible agony. The babe's eyes are closed, her mouth shaped like a flower bud, her skin lighter than Akaiyan's, but darker than mine. She has black hair.

"Is she... all right?"

"Perfect," smiles Mistress Steueens, "a most perfect babe if ever I saw one."

Sinopa leans over me, her eyes shining.

"Today, you have made the *unqua* happy," she says in her sing-song voice. "This is a day we will say, *oonutsauka*, I remember."

They leave me then, my babe tucked warm and snug next

to me. Mother has finished cleaning me and changing the sheets. She's brushed my hair the way she'd done for Eleanor after Virginia's birth.

"Thank you, sweet Jesus," she says through her tears, "for giving us this new life." She kisses me. "I'll send Akaiyan in. He wants to see his wife and child."

Dreamily, I give Akaiyan my hand. He kisses my cheek and pulls back the coverlet to see his new daughter.

"Are you... disappointed?"

"Why should I be?"

"Because I haven't given you a son."

"You have given me a child, a girl to love who is just like you. What more could I want?"

Then I'm left alone to rest. I'm exhausted from my labors and the child still sleeps quietly next to me. In my dream, Ananyas comes to me, and sweet little Agnes, looking at my babe and admiring her.

'You have a fine daughter,' says Ananyas, smiling down. 'She'll bring you much joy.'

'She'll be happiness for you,' whispers Agnes.

I reach out my hand to touch her cheek but she vanishes. I sleep without dreams after that.

Toward evening, my babe awakens and begins to cry lustily.

"Oh, Mother," I call in alarm. "Something's wrong with her."

Mother smiles.

"Nothing's wrong," she says. "She's hungry. Put her to your breast."

The babe suckles vigorously, her mouth working hard. What joy, to hold new life and feel it draw strength from me! I weep in my ecstasy. Akaiyan comes to see me, kissing my lips, my cheek, kissing our babe. He goes quietly and I fall asleep again. Mother stays all night and in the morning, Father himself comes to my bedside, leaning heavily upon my dear mother, to see his new grandchild. He kisses me and says a prayer. Then he takes the child and holds her for a few moments.

"What a beautiful babe," he whispers. "You've given us much joy, dear Jess."

"Oh, Father, I'm so glad... so very glad you're here."

He gives the babe back to me, then turns to go.

"What are you calling her?"

"For you and Mother, Suzanne Emily."

"And for you and Akaiyan?"

"Oohahn-ne."

He nods his head and blows me a kiss from his hand. I pretend to catch it in mine. My beloved father's eyes are shining, and I will always remember how he looks, for this is the last time I ever see him alive.

Chapter 31

Father's Death

I THINK OFTEN that the Great Spirit gave me such a beautiful child because He knew my father would have to go away. It makes things easier to bear. Holding Oohahn-ne in my arms gives me great comfort; knowing that Father got to see her before he died helps assuage my grief.

Mother discovers him the next morning cold in his bed, a smile upon his lips. Blood flecks the sheet from his terrible cough, but at least he's at peace. She doesn't weep, nor tear her hair. Thomas finds her sitting next to the bed, leaning her head upon his chest, his hand in hers. He runs to call Mistress Steueens, who comes and leads her back to my house. There, she busies herself with my little babe, holding and sponging her, rocking her while I sleep, keeping the sadness deep within her.

So I don't find out until later that day, when Akaiyan tells me, oh, so gently. Mother has left under the care of Mistress Steueens and Mistress Powell. Akaiyan is watching me change little Oohahn-ne, playing softly with her hair, stroking her tiny ears.

When he breaks the news, I stop for a moment, then continue swaddling my child. I place her searching mouth against my breast, feeling the suck and pull of her hunger. I begin to hum an old lullaby, from an almost-forgotten English past.

"Hush, hush, my little babe,
Mother is here, Father is near.
Hush, hush, sweet little babe,
God watches over you closely here."

The tears run silently down my cheeks, burying themselves in my nightgown. I don't even try to wipe them away. Akaiyan sits there, letting me cry, for he has come to understand *nickreruroh* tears. After a while, there are no more for the pain has dried them all up. Little Oohahn-ne has fallen asleep in the middle of her feeding. I shift her to my other breast; she wakes up and begins suckling again. Akaiyan leans over and kisses my cheek, kisses my uncovered breast.

"Your father was a good man," he says.

"Yes, a very good man."

"We shall miss him greatly."

I just nod my head, for words are not coming easily. I stare at my babe, then at Akaiyan. I sense the beauty of what is now mine: husband, child, father, daughter. I reach out my hand and touch his cheek.

"Little Bird," he whispers, "I grieve for you."

Oh, where have I heard those words before? Then I remember. I said them once to young George Howe after his father was murdered. 'Oh, George,' I said, 'I'm grieving for you,' throwing my arms about him.

What is pain, after all? The swelling of the throat until

one chokes? The ache in the heart that never stops? The physical pain of bringing Oohahn-ne into the world is nothing, nothing, compared to this! If I were cut with a thousand knives, if my blood ran from my body soaking into the earth, I could not feel more pain than I feel right now.

I remember Father, not as a sick man old before his time, but as young and vibrant, chopping wood, laughing around the supper table, winking at Mother when he thought no one was looking. I remember him holding her as they danced around the room, knowing they were finally sailing for the New World to make a new life for us all. I remember how many times he hugged me, comforted me, spoke words of great wisdom to me. I remember, I remember, and the pain doesn't stop.

Manteo himself comes to visit, touching the babe's tiny cheek with his finger, saying an *unqua* prayer over both of us.

"*Oonaquera, cotuch eets hitchra waure ki-yu-se*, a thousand times may the Great Spirit give you peace."

He sits with me for a long time, saying nothing, watching the babe. When she cries and I have to feed her, he neither looks away, nor acts embarrassed as I uncover my breast. In amazement, I realize that I'm not embarrassed either, for to suckle this *unqua* child, this child of love, is as natural as breathing air.

I rise from my birthing bed to attend the funeral services for my father. Though it's still winter and the ground hard, the men have managed to dig a place in the burying ground set aside for us. There, they take my dear father's body, washed and wrapped in white cloth. Roger Bayley says the prayers; Mother stands dry-eyed, only her lower lip trembling as we say farewell.

I walk to the grave holding Oohahn-ne. Taking the babe's

tiny hand in mine, I have her blow a kiss to my father. Oohahn-ne blows the kiss, but Suzanne Emily cries, her sad wails echoing the pain in all our hearts.

Chapter 32

In Mourning

"YOUR FATHER WAS my source of strength," Mother says one evening, not long after his funeral. We're sitting around the supper table at her house, for Thomas has asked that we all eat there, the sadness too much for him to handle.

I come with Akaiyan, Oohahn-ne and Quayah, who's just delighted to be included. He and Thomas are good friends, even more so since Quayah killed the Spanish intruder. Mother and I clear the dishes, while Akaiyan lights up his *oosquaana*. The smoke drifts toward the hole in the roof cut especially for that purpose.

"You're a strong woman, Mother. I believe that Father got his strength from you."

She smiles thinly, scraping the dishes and then scrubbing them vigorously. Impulsively, I lean my head against her shoulder.

"All I am, I learned from you."

"Well," she breaks into a laugh, "that must be true,

indeed. Your stubbornness, your... courage...."

"Am I courageous, then?"

"To do what you've done, to search for Ananyas, to lead Eleanor and the others into the wilderness, to... to marry...."

"No longer against your wishes, dear Mother?"

"No," she whispers, "no longer against my wishes. You made your father very happy. He saw his granddaughter. How many men can boast that?"

"And did I not make a sweet babe?"

"Indeed you did, Jess dear, the sweetest babe ever."

She glances with deep love toward Oohahn-ne, sleeping soundly in her little cradle. Already she's grown, her little cheeks fat and round. She's a hungry child, always willing to eat and now, sleeping through the night. What a blessing to be able to sleep uninterrupted. I've tried to see whom she looks like more, me or Akaiyan. She has my mouth, Mother says, but Akaiyan's strong chin. She wails like an English child, strong and determined to be fed, to be changed. But her darker complexion reveals her Indian heritage.

"She'll have the best of both worlds," I tell Mother but, for the first time, I see a shadow of doubt cross her face.

"Not the best English world," she whispers, "for we're all *unqua* here, it seems."

And that's true. As our English clothes wear out, the men and women turn to buckskin garb, *ough-tre's*, shirts and *oo-ross-soo*, shoes of soft deer hides. Some of the men have begun wearing feathers in their hair, letting it grow long and pulling it back in native fashion. The women gladly wear the shell necklaces, given as gifts by our friends. The hot sun and the sea winds have tanned our skins dark.

Several nights, I bring Oohahn-ne to my mother's lodge, leaving her there overnight since she sleeps so soundly. This

gives Akaiyan and me some time alone. We've begun making love again, soft and sweet, for my recovery from birthing has been complete and swift. Dear Eleanor, I sometimes think as I lie in the dark of our lodge house listening to Akaiyan's soft breathing, dear sweet Eleanor, I know now what you meant. To love a man is the sweetest of all possible things.

I think so often of my dear father that it's almost as if he's still alive, somewhere in the woods chopping timber, or building a new house across the village. I hear the men singing sometimes, or the voices of the women as they tend their hearths, and imagine my father singing in his strong, powerful voice. Only when I look at Mother do I realize, with deep sadness, that he's no longer with us, and how much she still grieves.

For they were still in love, all through the Atlantic crossing, the building of our colony on Roanoak, the settling on Croatoan Island. I could see it in their glances toward each other, their sweet smiles when they spoke of the other, their unashamed flirting when they thought Thomas and I weren't looking. I knew they still loved and delighted in that secret knowledge that my mother and father, after so many years, were like lovers in springtime. I think that my mother wouldn't trade those memories for a million lifetimes with a man she didn't love. I pray that my own marriage to Akaiyan will last as long. I pray for many more children like Oohahn-ne.

Mother spends a great deal of time at Father's grave site, reading his favorite passages from the Holy Bible, talking quietly to him. Perhaps he's there, after all, conversing with her. I firmly believe the spirit lives on and, even now, all those whom I've loved, who have died, smile down from Heaven upon us all.

The days pass rapidly, the snows melt slowly but steadily, and our world turns its face toward spring. Soon there'll be the time of Oohahn-ne's christening and a wedding to be planned, Enrique to Te-lah-tai.

Chapter 33

A Christening And A Wedding

THE VILLAGE BLOSSOMS with excitement. Today's the day of my babe's christening. Tomorrow, Enrique and Te-lah-tai will wed. In addition, two of the *unqua* women who've recently had babes have asked to be a part of the christening ceremony. It's a time of great joy.

Manteo gives his blessing upon the three infants. Sinopa will participate in the Christian ceremony, speaking words in English which I've taught her. And Roger Bayley has learned an Indian prayer, to say over all three *utserosta*. With Te-lah-tai's help, I've fashioned a christening outfit for Oohahn-ne. To please Mother, she'll be wrapped in a shawl of purest white lace, Mother's own.

The day blesses us with fair weather and a sweet soft breeze blowing inland from the sea. We stand in the open air in the center of the village, where all ceremonies take place, listening to the sounds of the babes' whimpering as precious Holy Water is sprinkled upon their foreheads.

"Bless these children, Oh Jesus Christ, Oh Great Spirit," intones Sinopa, with great difficulty pronouncing the English words, "for they come to offer you their hearts, their spirits. Love and bless them and keep them safe."

Nickreruroh and *unqua* both shed tears of joy. Like our good friends, we stamp our feet gently in approval.

"*Oonaquera, cotuch eets hitchra waure ki-yu-se,*" says Roger Bayley, saying the same words Manteo said to me after the birth, though he stumbles also over the strange sounds: "A thousand times may the Great Spirit give you peace."

Then he surprises us all.

"*Ne unche, ne wartsauh, e youch se, tichke oonaquera ee hitchra waure koone-hah,* not one, not ten, but a hundred blessings upon all, in the eyes of our Great Spirit."

We all break in cheers, stamping our feet loudly. Che-Chou and Sooka woof their approval and from the *a hots'* shelter, a round of neighing.

The next day, the weather is equally fair. Our Good Lord blesses all in the sweet sunlight, the deep blue of the sky. Enrique, dressed in finest *wahunshe*, breeches, and *ough-tre's* of buckskin, stands beside Te-lah-tai in her prettiest dress of *ocques*. Necklaces of copper and shells adorn her bodice. She's all smiles as the marriage ceremony is performed, first in Croatoan, then English, finally in Spanish. It's Carlos who does the honors in the Spanish tongue, asking God's blessing on their union and that it might prove fertile.

"Oh, great *Jesús Cristo*, we ask your blessing upon the joining of Enrique and Te-lah-tai, that your light will always shine upon them, that they may know no sorrow, and that they have *muchos hijos*."

Enrique blushes under his tan when Carlos says that, then leans over and whispers something to Te-lah-tai. She, too, blushes. In *unqua*, I translate for her mother, Ro-yaa-reh, who begins clapping her hands loudly. Then I translate in English for Mother, Thomas and the others. They begin to clap. Soon the entire entourage is stamping its feet and clapping. Enrique sweeps Te-lah-tai into his arms, kissing her most passionately. Ro-yaa-reh punches Enrique in the arm and gives a broad wink.

"*Tewots utserosta*," she says again and again, "many children."

The potent beer is once more passed around the village. The celebrations go on all afternoon and into the evening. At dusk, Enrique leads Te-lah-tai to their newly-constructed house, just as Akaiyan had once led me. I feel his great joy, giving both him and his bride a warm hug.

"Go in peace," I whisper in Spanish and Croatoan. They nod their heads and run off. Loud whistles and whoops follow them. When the door flap closes on their privacy, a tremendous hollering begins. I think they must have done this for Akaiyan and me but we hardly heard, so filled were we with passion, our eyes and ears only for the other.

There's much dancing well into the night. I finally put Oohahn-ne to sleep in her cradle, leaving Mother to watch her. Then Akaiyan and I join in the festivities, dancing, singing and laughing. Even Thomas is allowed to stay up late. I see him and Quayah sipping beer; I start to frown, then turn away. They're almost men, after all. In a few more years, our Thomas may stand before the village with a bride of his own. I look around, wondering who that might be. There are several young maidens of about fourteen, some younger by only a few years. One of them might be my new sister-in-law some day. I rock back and forth, thinking of the possibilities. Today is a day filled with happiness and expectation. We are one with the *unqua* now, and there's much peace in my heart.

Later that night, Akaiyan holds me in his arms, whispering words of sweetness and love. Little Oohahn-ne stirs in her sleep and I reach out to rock the cradle. I haven't told him yet of the new life which has taken hold in my womb. Though I'm still nursing Oohahn-ne, life has unexpectedly begun and God's miracle of love blossoms and awakens with sweet mystery.

Chapter 34

Chaunoctay's Foal

WENEFRID POWELL ANNOUNCES that she, too, is expecting a child again. And so are Jane Jones, wife of Griffen, and Emme Colman, wife of Thomas. Our *nickreruroh* clan is matching the *unqua*, child for child. In addition to the two new babes baptized with Oohahn-ne, two of the Indian women are pregnant also. They are Ousrahti and Soo-kahche. They laugh and giggle a great deal, matching the size of their bellies as the babes grow and begin to move. Mother jokes and says it must be the sweet water, or the fresh air, or something!

Only Akaiyan knows I'm expecting again, the joy in his face when I tell him a wondrous sight, indeed. He kneels before me and places his head against my belly.

"I can hear it," he says most earnestly.

"Indeed not," I laugh, "only my stomach gurgling."

My child will be born in March of the year of Our Lord, 1591. There's still no word from John White. Several of our men rowed back to Roanoak last week, to see if he'd yet returned. They reported sadly that all was still the same, the ruins in more disrepair than ever.

Our village grows in size, the lodge houses expanding out from the open center like rings in the trunk of a tree. Enrique and Te-lah-tai's is the farthest, almost to the tree line. Enrique says he likes it that way. He's built another shelter for the *a hots*, for our herd expands. We now have nine in number, including Star and Hoonoch who continue to grow. And today, Chaunoctay goes into labor and delivers another girl horse, *"una hembra,"* Enrique says, smiling broadly.

Like Beauty and Fawn, Chaunoctay's labor is easy. Unlike the birth of human children, the *a hots* don't seem to suffer. Enrique tells me, however, that back in *España* he saw several still-births and one mare who had to be cut open and her foal taken that way. She died, most unfortunately, and they had to feed the *potrico* milk from another mare. So even animals can have their troubles.

Chaunoctay's pangs are mild and within an hour, the little *hembra* slips into our world. Enrique and Carlos quickly help clean her up, then she stands on her feet and begins to suckle right away. We all cheer. For every new life is a victory over death and we bless the animals as do the *unqua*, sharing this beautiful land with them in harmony.

Carlos is given the honor of choosing a name. The filly is a deep bay in color, for Thunderer is her father. He thinks for several moments, then decides.

"We'll call her Roja, for the red color of wine."

"How do you know about wine?" Enrique teases him. Carlos blushes but won't tell.

Ro-yaa-reh, Te-lah-tai's mother, comes often to the *a hots'* shelter, to admire Chaunoctay's new foal. But she doesn't like the name Carlos has chosen. She stamps her foot and says, "no," most emphatically.

"You name her," I say then.

"Cotcoo-rea," she nods her head.

"Red," I whisper to Carlos and Enrique, and we all grin behind her back.

Enrique quarters Beauty and Star, Fawn and Hoonoch and Utchar in the compound he's built. Chaunoctay, Cotcoo-rea, and Qui-heiratse stay with Diablo. We've had to build a separate shelter just for Thunderer, for he and Diablo don't like each other still. And now Qui-heiratse has come into her season. She swings her tail to one side and pushes up against Diablo. He's very obliging and before long, Qui-heiratse is carrying his foal.

Manteo is most admiring of the *a hots*. He knows they'll carry his people far and wide, gathering food and hunting for game. I'm sure there are other tribes who've managed to capture Spanish *caballos* and have seen their potential, just like we have. Certainly, the Neusiok have one already. If I close my eyes, I can imagine great herds of horses carrying the *unqua* all over, covering great distances in one day. I can picture the clouds of dust raised by their flying hooves, the sound like thunder echoing in my ears. This land will one day be a land of *unqua* and *a hots* together, joined as one, making their mark upon the Kingdom of God, upon the world of the Great Spirit.

I kiss little Cotcoo-rea on her soft nose, watching her stumble unsteadily about the stall. Chaunoctay, like Beauty and Fawn, is a good mother, licking her babe, cuddling her close. The peace and tranquility of the horses is like a balm to my soul. I lean back against the rough wood wall, watching the *hembra*, listening to the soft sounds of the mare, the snorting of great Diablo. Che-Chou plays at my feet, tugging on my *oo-ross-soo*. He rips one and suddenly tumbles back, rolling over and looking very surprised. A torn piece of deerskin dangles from his mouth.

"Oh, silly boy," I laugh. "Now I'll have to make another pair."

He comes padding over to me and I rub his fur. Little Che-Chou is like a dog now. He sits and stays when told. Sooka, likewise, keeps my mother company and, wonder of wonders, is allowed to sleep at the foot of her bed. He rests with one of dear Father's shirts always between his paws.

Chapter 35

Teaching School

SEVERAL OF THE WOMEN have come to my lodge begging me to continue what Eleanor started, teaching school to the little ones. So I've decided to do just that, become a teacher like my dear friend. It will help keep her close to my heart.

She left me all the slates and markers for the little ones. I entreat Mother to watch Oohahn-ne while I teach the lessons: the sums, the writing, the reading of our Holy Scriptures. Some of the women come also, sitting in the back of the room while I talk about adding and subtracting, often using berries and nuts instead of abstract marks upon a slate. As a reward, the children are allowed to eat their correct answers but, if incorrect, they must rework the problems. Most of the time, each one is correct. I keep Akaiyan, Carlos and Enrique busy gathering more nuts and berries, for my students are consuming them quickly.

For writing, we practice scratching our names upon the rough slate, remembering capital letters for the first names.

The *unqua* don't have last names, it seems, so I haven't bothered teaching those. Then I teach them simple sentences to write, like "Who is that big dog over there?" and "How are you feeling today?"

For fun, we practice acting out the words we've written. The children learn quickly and the mothers clap their hands. When I read from the Holy Bible they love to listen to the Book of Ruth, or Ecclesiastes, my dear father's favorite. Sometimes I tell them the story of Adam and Eve, and of Cain and Abel.

"And Cain talked with Abel his brother: and it came to pass, when they were in the field, that Cain rose up against Abel his brother, and slew him. And the Lord said unto Cain, 'Where is Abel thy brother?' And he said, 'I cannot tell, am I my brother's keeper?' "

The *unqua* women nod their heads, but I'm not sure they understand. Enrique is standing in the doorway when he overhears me. A look of pain comes upon his face and he rushes from my house. I turn to Wenefrid Powell, who gladly takes over the lesson as I rush after Enrique.

"What's the matter?" I ask.

His face is buried in his hands.

"Dear Enrique, tell me, please."

"I, too... have killed *mis hermanos....*"

"Why? What do you mean?"

And then, I realize. He has slain Spanish *soldados*, when we fled the garrison, when we took *los caballos*. Oh, how thoughtless of me to quote that exact passage from God's Holy Scriptures about brothers, when I knew he was listening.

"Enrique, I'm so sorry. Will you forgive me?"

He lifts his face from his hands and stares at me.

"There's no need to forgive you. It's I who must ask God's

forgiveness."

He turns to walk away.

"Enrique, Jesus Christ forgives us all, for none are without sin."

He stops then, and I walk to him.

"Come back," I entreat, "come back and be healed."

He follows me back to the lodge, his mouth set in a line of pain, his eyes wet with tears. Oh, what can I read to him that he'll understand, to ease his heart, to free his soul from its torment? I thumb quickly through the pages.

"Let him that is among you without sin cast the first stone...." from John 8:7.

"Father forgive them, for they know not what they do...." from Luke 23:34.

"Ask and it shall be given you. Seek and ye shall find. Knock, and it shall be opened unto you...." from Matthew 7:7.

I read until my mouth is dry and my voice begins to tremble. The little ones and their mothers are enthralled. But more important, Enrique's anguish is gone. I can see it in his eyes. He stays after everyone leaves. I go and embrace him.

"You have so much goodness in you, God is surely not angry for what you did, what you had to do."

"You've given me peace, little Jess," he says, using the term my father always used. "I give thanks to *Jesús Cristo por nuestra amistad*, our friendship."

He crosses himself and I do the same. No matter how Indian we may be, or yet become, our belief in Our Lord and Savior will never diminish. Enrique leaves my lodge house with his head up and his heart free. And I, who always think only of myself, have learned a valuable lesson. We can't always see the pain of others, but we must never forget how they may suffer in silence.

Chapter 36

Coins Of Silver And Gold

"COULD WE EVER get back to *España*?" Carlos asks Enrique while we're tending the a hots. Cotcoo-rea is suckling, her whisk of a tail moving back and forth.

"It's not likely," he replies, grooming Diablo with the stalk brush. Diablo groans in his pleasure and we all smile.

"What if a Spanish ship weighs anchor near here. Could we get to her? Could we pay our way with the coins?"

"If she comes close, she'll likely be dashed upon the shoals, as before."

Carlos's face sinks.

"What waits for you back *en España, mi amigo?*"

He shrugs.

"No real *familia*, I suppose. My parents are dead, so that's why I ran away to sea. And what of you?"

"Once, a long time ago, I wanted to return. But now...," he smiles, "now I don't wish it anymore. For I have Te-lah-tai...."

Carlos and I smile broadly. For Enrique has been silly in love ever since his wedding day. Everyday I expect news of a babe, though nothing's happened yet. But if they had a babe for every time the entrance to their lodge swung closed, they'd be knee-deep in little ones.

"And what of you?" Enrique asks. "For there are pretty maidens all around."

Carlos blushes.

"I'm not ready for that."

"Indeed not," I say most vigorously. "For he's only twelve, much too young."

"Almost thirteen," he corrects me.

"Still too young," I laugh, reaching out to box his ears. He darts away and begins playing with Che-Chou.

We all know of the silver and gold coins the men brought back from the stranded ship. The box was heavy in its weight and when the men pried open the rusted lock, we all gasped. For it was thick with coins, doubloons of purest gold, silver shining in the sun. Roger Bayley and the others thought it must have been bounty from a plundered ship. The box was stored for safe-keeping in his house, though no one had a thought to steal it. For gold and silver buys nothing in this world of ours, not good health, nor long life, nor happiness.

Thomas has been initiated into the group of *quottis*. A special ceremony was held, with Manteo officiating. He was stripped of all *ocques* down to a loincloth, then his body painted with various symbols in bold reds, blues and browns, each one depicting an animal spirit. Manteo gave him a list of tasks to undertake. He had to go away into the woodlands for seven days and nights, living only by his wits and his ability to hunt game. Mother wasn't happy but he's *unqua* now, so she sighed and went about her daily tasks with a heavy heart.

There's much rejoicing when he finally returns, for it's been the longest week of our lives. He left a boy and comes back a man. Manteo tells him he can no longer live in his mother's house, but must dwell with the other *quottis* in a communal lodge. He's been allowed to pick out a new name and from now on, he's asked us to call him Cauhau-wean, wildcat. I'm thankful that Mother has Sooka for company. Wenefrid Powell spends a great deal of time with her, and she goes often to the Powell lodge. Mistress Steueens is mother to us all as usual and, much to her dismay, has finally run out of sweet honey for her teas. She must have packed jars and jars of it when we first left England so long ago, but her supply is now exhausted. Today, Akaiyan, Quayah and Carlos are going with Manteo to gather more honey from the swarms of bees that live amidst the trees.

They go off into the woods, armed with nothing more than nets on long poles and buckets to place the honeycombs in. The *nickreruroh* women have prepared poultices just in case of bee stings, but the *unqua* haven't. They laugh at our concern and go about their business. Te-lah-tai whispers to me that a special oil has been rubbed into the men's skins which the bees don't like.

"So no one will be stung," she smiles.

I tell Mother so she won't worry.

"I declare," she says, breathing a sigh of relief, "the *unqua* have so many mysterious ways...."

They come back several hours later, laden with combs dripping with nature's own goodness. None of them have been stung, not even once. Mistress Steueens clucks and giggles over the new supply of honey. She's become quite adept at brewing native teas which are stronger and slightly more bitter, and will definitely be improved with the addition of the golden syrup.

I watch the men ladle the honey out of the buckets, stripping the combs of the succulent liquid. I suddenly think of all the gold and silver lying in a rusted chest in Master Bayley's lodge. No wonder the *unqua* have no use for such coins. Their gold comes from the honeybee, their silver from the moonlight which paints the sand and the trees, the grassy dunes and the sea. I smell the salt breeze which blows from across the waters. There's life in that freshened wind. Mother now knows of my expectant child. She kisses me and weeps copious tears; she holds me and laughs, then weeps again. The circle of life moves ever onward.

Chapter 37

Reflections

LITTLE OOHAHN-NE is such a good child. She sleeps all night long; she now follows me with her eyes and even smiles at the sound of my voice. I carry her upon my back the way the *unqua* women do, wrapped snugly in a carrier attached with straps. She sleeps comforted by the warmth of my body and the muffled beat of my heart.

Sadness still veils Mother like a mantle, but with Oohahn-ne, she smiles and sings the old lullabies. What a rich heritage she brings my *utserosta*, my babe, and now in eagerness I listen to the stories Sinopa tells with a new ear and a new understanding. For each story is a tale rich in tradition: how Mother Earth began, how the stars and moon came about, why the tortoise moves so slowly, how the porcupine got his quills, why the *squarrena* howl at night. These songs and stories I'll pass on to Suzanne Emily, to Oohahn-ne, and she'll be the richer for both.

Carlos and Enrique have formed a fast friendship, like

blood brothers. And now Carlos and Quayah are often together, hunting, fishing, one teaching, the other learning the
unqua ways.

When Roger Bayley tells us that some of the Spanish
coins have been removed from the old, rusted chest in his
lodge, we're all amazed. For what good will coins do us here?
There are no goods to buy. The land gives us its bounty freely
and without reserve. The earth asks only that we nurture and
take care of her, like loving guardians are supposed to do.

A thought crosses my mind that perhaps Carlos has taken
them, to try and buy passage home to *España* should the
opportunity ever arise. Then I immediately feel guilty and
shake my head. For he seems an honest youth, eager to learn
and willing to do his fair share of the work. He's gentle and
kind with *los caballos*, sweet to Che-Chou and Sooka, and like
a cousin to Oohahn-ne. I'm distressed that I'd even think such
a thought.

He's told us he has no *familia* back home, and has
attached himself to Enrique and Te-lah-tai like glue. Many
times they have to chase him from their house so they can
have some privacy. On those occasions, he goes to Mother's
house, to keep her company now that Cauhau-wean sleeps in
the *quottis* lodge house, following the manhood traditions.
Discipline is strict for those young braves; early to bed and
up at dawn, learning and toiling until sunset. There are
rigorous survival games and little time for relaxation.

In accordance with *unqua* tradition, mothers-in-law
aren't supposed to enter their son-in-law's house unless
strictly invited. However, Akaiyan knows of my desire to see
much of my dear mother, so he graciously extends the invita-
tion. As I'm learning from him so he, too, learns from me.

Then Master Bayley tells us that more coins are missing,

so the mystery grows. Carlos laughs and seems happy, whether with Enrique, Quayah or around the rest of us. Perhaps too happy, I wonder? I've said nothing to anyone, not even Akaiyan. I can't bear the thought that our new little friend might be a thief.

And then, the mystery solves itself. Several of the little children, six and seven-year-olds, are seen playing with the coins at the edge of the village. They've been using them to throw, seeing who can reach the farthest target, or inventing their own game similar to playing with dice, tossing the coins high in the air; if the heads come up, a prize is won; if tails, then the loser must pay a forfeit. They're roundly scolded by Manteo and Sinopa, chastised by their mothers and the coins returned to Roger Bayley's care, whose lodge is placed off-limits to the *woccanookne*. This is the one restriction those little ones seem to have, for children wander freely in our village in and out the houses, loved and cherished by all.

I'm so relieved that when Carlos stops by to see little Oohahn-ne, I give him an extra hug. I don't tell him, nor will I ever.

Summer is in its fullest beauty. Hunting is good and we eat plentifully of the land's bounty, varying it with many fish from the sea. Maize grows tall in the fields; the squash and beans are yielding good crops. The *unqua* are good cultivators and now, excellent horsemen. Often we hold races to see who is the most agile, the most skilled. Quayah wins often, as does my dear brother, Cauhau-wean. I'm so proud.

Today I walk to the burial ground set aside for us. There I stop to reflect on the richness of my life here. I've gathered flowers to place on dear Father's grave, and some to put on the grave of Eleanor and Ananyas's tiny unborn babe. At this moment of deep contemplation, the tears fill my eyes most easily and I let them run, unchecked, down my cheeks. I hold Oohahn-ne out before me, showing my father his beloved granddaughter. I tell him softly of the new life beginning in my womb. How happy he must be, his spirit seeing all.

"Dearest Father, may you rest in peace forever and ever."

Oohahn-ne gives a sudden little laugh, which makes me smile also. I tickle her nose and fat cheeks with a purple flower. She reaches to grab it. I hear the sounds of the birds and the whirring of the many insects, all living in peace. From my vantage point, I can see the deep blue of the sea stretching out to its limitless distance, the sea of life which once I feared to cross. It's brought me here to this beautiful land, to this endless happiness with Akaiyan.

And then on the horizon, I see something which makes my blood freeze in my veins. A ship approaches but whether English or Spanish, I don't know. I can't make out its flag, for it's still too far away. For a moment I'm rooted to the ground. Then I pick Oohahn-ne up in my arms and run back to the village as fast as I can.

"A ship, a ship," I cry, and everyone comes out to see.

Chapter 38

Ship In Disguise

THE MEN OF THE VILLAGE gather their firearms, their bows and arrows, and send a group to see if they can tell what ship it is. Some of the *nickreruroh* seem pleased, for an English ship would signal that rescue has finally arrived.

Carlos is hoping for a Spanish vessel, "One big enough to take me and Enrique and *los caballos* back to *España.*"

But Enrique shakes his head, holding tightly to Te-lah-tai's hand. As much as he wants to see his dear mother and sisters, he loves Te-lah-tai and wouldn't leave her.

Mother, who once wanted to return to English soil, now seems reluctant to venture out of her lodge house. If she were to return to England, she'd leave behind a beloved husband buried, a dear son, daughter and granddaughter who are now Indian.

As for me... as for me, I have no desire to return to the English life I left so long ago, the hustle and bustle of a world full of materialistic things. My home is here, and here I wish to stay.

Good news comes soon. For it's an English vessel, flying the English flag of Tudor. At least we're safe from the Spanish, I think to myself, not wanting to hurt Carlos's feelings. For the Spanish would, indeed, plunder this sweet village and take their *caballos* back with them.

While we wait for the English to anchor out beyond the shoals and send small boats in, I walk to the *a hots'* shelter, to spend some precious time with them. As I enter the familiar place, the rich smell and the soft sounds fill my very soul. Always, I'm at peace here with the animals. I find them close to God, close to the Great Spirit. Their strong bodies belie their sweet, gentle natures. Diablo, Chaunoctay and Qui-hei-ratse whinny greetings when they see me and the little one, Cotcoo-rea, comes trotting over.

"Oh, sweet darling," I whisper, petting her, "how I love you."

I show Oohahn-ne the foal, taking her tiny hand and placing it on the sleek neck, stroking her with her little fingers. She laughs and chuckles and rocks back and forth on my lap.

Who knows how long a time I spend there, lost in a world of loveliness and innocence. Che-Chou is curled at my feet, content just to lie close. Suddenly, he gives a low growl and stands, stiff-legged. But it's only Akaiyan who slips inside, so he relaxes.

"You must come with me," my husband whispers urgently. "Do not ask questions. Come now."

"What is it?"

He puts a finger to his lips, gathering Oohahn-ne in his arms.

"Quickly, quickly. Into the woods behind us. Enrique

and Te-lah-tai are waiting."

"But what...?"

He doesn't answer, pushing me ahead of him out the entrance and away from the village toward the trees.

"Akaiyan?"

"Go, go, do not stop, do not ask questions."

A terrible fear has suddenly gripped me. I take Oohahn-ne from him and we run as fast as we can, deep into the woods. Che-Chou runs alongside, silent, sensing the urgency. Oh, where is Mother? Where is Cauhau-wean, Carlos, and all the rest?

We run until we can run no more. Oohahn-ne starts to whimper, but I quickly put her to my breast and she quiets down. We see Enrique and Te-lah-tai crouching near some bushes.

"What's happening?" I ask frantically.

"Didn't he tell you?"

I shake my head, too scared to hear what I think I might hear.

"It's a pirate ship, not English. They flew a false flag to trick us. It's a pirate ship and their boats have just landed at the eastern beach. Manteo and the others are gathering at the dunes to fight them."

"Pirates!" I tremble, thinking for a moment of a long-forgotten face, that of the rogue Simon Fernandes, who left us stranded on Roanoak almost three years ago. Pirates, those villainous, black-bearded men who owe allegiance to no country, who pillage the seas and take whatever they want. No one is safe from them, English, Spanish, certainly not *unqua*.

"I want to go and fight them," Enrique says suddenly, standing up. "For I'm no coward."

Te-lah-tai begins to cry.

"You can not," Akaiyan places his hand on Enrique's arm. "There are too many. Manteo, himself, told me to leave even though I wanted to stay. He said to get my wife and child and come here. He said to tell you to hide, also."

And so we wait hidden deep in the trees, wondering what will happen to our village, to our friends? And what of the *a hots*, of Sooka, of the small children, the babes? I want to cry but can't, thinking only that a few short hours ago paradise was mine and now, the world that I know and love is about to vanish.

Epilogue

THOUGH THE PERIOD between 1587 and 1590 does not reveal what happened to The Lost Colony, it is probable that both Spanish explorers and pirates continued sailing up and down the eastern seaboard, sometimes anchoring their ships and landing. Across the sea in England, the period between 1590 and 1607 was a time of great turmoil. Elizabeth I died in 1603 and James I succeeded to the throne. Men of power concentrated on getting monetary backing and royal endorsement for yet more expeditions to the New World.

The pirate ship which landed at Croatoan Island is purely fiction. However, it could have happened just that way, leaving the reader to speculate upon the events yet to come.

More adventures lie in store for Jess in the fourth book of The Lyon Saga...

The Lyon's Throne

Jess and her friends return to England where they are swept up against their will in the turmoil of Elizabeth's court. Jess must use her wits to survive and plan for the day she can sail back to Croatoan Island and her peaceful life.

FURTHER READING

Daniell, David, Editor. *Tyndale's New Testament*. New Haven & London: Yale University Press, 1989.

————. *Tyndale's Old Testament*. New Haven & London: Yale University Press, 1989.

Durant, David N. *Ralegh's Lost Colony: The Story of the First English Settlement in America*. New York: Atheneum, 1981.

Hawke, David. *The Colonial Experience*. New York: Bobbs-Merrill Co. Inc., 1966.

Hoffman, Paul E. *Spain and the Roanoke Voyages*. Raleigh: North Carolina Dept. of Cultural Resources, Division of Archives and History, 1987.

Humber, John L. *Backgrounds and Preparations for the Roanoke Voyages, 1584-1590*. Raleigh: North Carolina Dept. of Cultural Resources, Division of Archives and History, 1986.

Kupperman, Karen Ordahl. *Roanoke, The Abandoned Colony*. Maryland: Rowman and Littlefield, 1984.

Lawson, John. *A New Voyage to Carolina*. Chapel Hill: University of North Carolina, 1967.

Miller, Helen Hill. *Passage to America: Ralegh's Colonists Take Ship for Roanoke*. Raleigh: North Carolina Dept. of Cultural Resources, Division of Archives and History, 1983.

Perdue, Theda. *Native Carolinians: The Indians of North Carolina*. Raleigh: North Carolina Dept. of Cultural Resources, Division of Archives and History, 1985.

Quinn, David Beers. *The Lost Colonists: Their Fortune and Probable Fate*. Raleigh: North Carolina Dept. of Cultural Resources, Division of Archives and History, 1984.

—. *Set Fair For Roanoke: Voyages and Colonies, 1584-1606.* Chapel Hill: University of North Carolina Press, 1985.

Quinn, David B. & Alison Quinn. *The First Colonists: Documents on the Planting of the First English Settlements In North America, 1584-1590.* Raleigh: North Carolina Dept. of Cultural Resources, Division of Archives and History, 1982.

Rights, Douglas L. *The American Indian in North Carolina.* Winston-Salem: John F. Blair, 1991.

Stick, David. *Roanoke Island: The Beginnings of English America.* Chapel Hill: University of North Carolina, 1983.

M.L. Stainer

The author, having fallen in love with North Carolina's Outer Banks, decided to research the early colony that once existed on Roanoke Island. What mysterious circumstances led them to disappear? The Lyon Saga books explore many possibilities as to what may have happened to those brave men, women and children. M.L. Stainer weaves fact and fiction into fascinating history. Educated in London and at Fordham University, she lives in upstate New York with her husband, Frank, and numerous dog and cat family members.

James Melvin

James Melvin always dreamed of becoming an artist. He received his formal training from North Carolina's A & T State University in 1970. For several years this degree was put to use while James served as a Peace Corps art instructor in Botswana, Africa. Presently, James lives on the Outer Banks of North Carolina where he operates Melvin's Studio and Gallery. He is well-known for his stunning portrayals of black culture and simple treasures of life. A versatile artist, he works in oils, acrylics and pastels and has illustrated more than 20 children's books. His works are owned by collectors and art lovers throughout the U.S. and abroad.